# ADVENTURES
## OF A LIFETIME

M. LAWRENCE MOORE

Adventures of a Lifetime
Copyright © 2022 by M. Lawrence Moore

All rights reserved. No part of this publication may be reproduced,
distributed, or transmitted in any form or by any means, including
photocopying, recording, or other electronic or mechanical
methods, without the prior written permission of the author, except
in the case of brief quotations embodied in critical reviews and
certain other non-commercial uses permitted by copyright law.

ISBN
978-1-956529-86-9 (Paperback)
978-1-956529-85-2 (eBook)

# TABLE OF CONTENTS

# A CERTAIN MAN

There was a certain man who had a certain wife—a very certain wife. He sat in the shade of a fig tree, the first tree they had planted at the house they had bought as newlyweds long ago. He thought about her. He could do little physically on this hot day as he reminisced about their life together. He thought of how sure she was of things and how wonderful that was—usually.

Their parents had arranged the marriage but certainly not this house. When they were newlyweds, it was a stone ruin at the edge of town halfway up a steep rocky hill and for sale. She had stood just to the side of the seller on that very hot day so long ago. Three times the seller had named a price, and twice she had closed her eyes for not much longer than it takes to blink or to give her negative opinion silently. Twice her husband had watched her face and shaken his head from side to side. The third time the seller watched the man's eyes so he would not look at his wife and named the price he had in mind from the start. This time the husband was watching the animals foraging a little way up the hill. The husband said, "Yes, but we need the three goats and the burro and some lumber to repair the roof."

The seller was handsome, with a huge grin that displayed perfect, square teeth, a merchant of rugs and textiles with an extensive territory. He was very rich and, at first, did not care if he sold this rock pile and ruined house or not. He enjoyed haggling and finally arriving at an agreed price where he looked slightly generous. His recent instructions from home were clear and straightforward. "I do not care what you sell that rubble for. We are very comfortable and do not need it, but if you come home with those goats or that burro, you will sleep outside with them."

Nabil thought of his own very comfortable bed and thought of how the young couple needed the animals. He thought of how pleased he was that they wanted the animals and how they had bargained for them. In silent gratitude for the peace he would have at his own house, he determined to have his son, an architect, make the roof repairs extend at the back to create a shaded courtyard with room for the planting of fruit trees. The design would take advantage of any evening breeze after a day's work.

The very certain bride knew she had just given up her entire dowry and was still satisfied. From the small line of dark green plants along a seam in the rock beside the neglected house where the animals were grazing, she knew that the hill contained a tiny spring that would water her future plants and trees. To make sure the seller was satisfied as well, she spoke very quietly to her husband. "Please tell our new friend that he and his family will be honored guests in our home when it is ready."

Normally, after any transaction of consequence in or around the town, the terms of the sale were painfully and cleverly extracted from buyer and seller and then reworked and repeated with malice by a few of the residents until the parties bitterly regretted the arrangements and resented the opposing party.

In this case, the seller occasionally appeared in the town store with goat cheese and shared it with those who admitted how really good it was. In the first cold weather after the sale, Nabil wore a mohair sweater spun and knitted by the buyer's wife, Rebecca. By then, the townspeople were beginning to think he had done well.

Gabriel, the buyer, consulted with him about which fig trees were best, and they agreed on two American varieties—Black Mission from California's Franciscan mission farms and Brown Turkey. In America, at least, the second variety originated from beside a slave's cabin in the deep South. Grapevines and olive trees followed after consultation with Nabil as the terracing of the hill behind the house slowly progressed.

The fruits of their gardens were made available at reasonable prices at the small town's market, partly to be neighborly and partly to show the young couple had gotten a fair deal from their friend, Nabil.

Gabriel worked as a harvester of pistachios for the local growers. After the first year, he agreed to be paid for some of the work with a percentage of the crop and began assisting in negotiations for exported crops. He paid close attention to Nabil's business practices and never let a buyer leave angry. Twice he had called a buyer back and sweetened a deal that was already complete by offering an ample supply of figs and olives and vegetables from his gardens. He began to be a buyer of local produce and an exporter.

Very slowly during the first year, a four-foot-high rock wall was built parallel to the rear of the house about thirty feet back. With their own hands and with the help of the burro to carry stones in leather saddlebags, they carved a wide, crescent-shaped path from the town road below to the covered area built by Nabil's son at the rear of the house. The area between the house and the rock wall was leveled and paved with the smoothest stones. The extra rubble went behind the first wall, mixed with leaves and sand from dunes outside of town. The young burro was indispensable. The second and third walls took longer because of Gabriel's work and Rebecca's first and second pregnancy.

With the advice of Nabil, the merchant, and against the advice of the amateurs, specially chosen grapevines were planted in dirt and stone rubble and eventually produced fine wine. Today Rebecca thought their struggles, like the poor soil making richer wine, had made their life together richer. Mostly. But something was bothering Gabriel lately.

They had grown old together, he a little faster than she. He sat in his wicker chair in the garden and was only able to watch her work. She carried water from the well to their plants and trees in an ancient bucket, starting at the highest level. Year by year, they had terraced the hillside with sturdy rock walls and filled in behind each level with sand and soil carried in strong native baskets. There was a set of stone steps at one end of the terraced walls. The husband designed a cleared area before each wall so the next terrace could be worked and watered from the area before the wall with no bending down. She was most grateful for her husband's foresight. They had a few olive trees and many grapevines and cucumbers and tomatoes and every vegetable imaginable. His chair was in the shade of the Brown Turkey fig tree with a long, rough table beside it made from the old roof timbers that were salvaged. His clay cup and a jug of well water were at hand.

She watered the top level of the garden. As she emptied the bucket each trip, she gathered a few vegetables and set them on the table beside his chair. She was certain of the man her parents had chosen for her. She was certain of the success they had made of what had begun as a very humble house. As she toiled, he selected which vegetables would be used for dinner. She was certain of something else.

Her work today did not distract her from the fact that her husband was agitated. Of that, she was certain. When she had gathered enough vegetables for themselves and for barter with their neighbors and gifts for Nabil's family, she sat in another of the wicker chairs that surrounded the table. The four empty chairs were for their children who were married and lived away but often visited.

She waited a long time for him to formulate his thoughts and speak. He seemed to need her silent companionship to work out his thoughts. These last few weeks, she had seen him thrash and twitch in his sleep, never entirely at ease. Finally, today he spoke to her of his dreams and agitation.

Their children were the source of his troubled sleep. As he aged, he became uncertain and worried whether he had taught them to follow the ways of the One Who had made them each. He recently began to have a recurring dream. He appeared before the Eternal Tribunal and was being asked if he could account for his children's training.

The very certain wife absorbed the facts and then sat quietly until he finally said, "Well?"

"Are you planning on having a family gathering?"

Until she asked, he did not know what he wanted, but now it became clear to him. "Yes, a family gathering."

Letters went out, and letters with excuses came back. In a strong tone dictated by the husband but written by the wife, all excuses were overruled.

A certain date was set, and, on that day, the couple's four children from near and far arrived. Their respective spouses were invited but did not come. Two sons and two daughters arrived in the town at different times throughout that day, and the townspeople who knew them would have paid to know the reason for this gathering. Their vehicles were left on the town road at the bottom of the hill. There was now electricity, and the children assumed it came from the town. Gabriel and Rebecca had their small joke about it and agreed to "leave them in the dark" about how Rebecca had hired civil engineering students recommended by Nabil's son, the architect, to install solar panels on the roof. The children, at least the older son, would not have believed their mother or any woman capable of being intelligent.

The children still had their rooms, and now there was more food than ever from the garden. What the garden did not produce was obtained through bartering at the town store or from neighbors by trading the extra figs and olives and vegetables which were abundant. The alfalfa in the garden was of no direct use to them beyond the old burro's small needs, but the neighbor's chickens grazed freely on the alfalfa, which gave them calcium and made their eggshells stronger and which entitled Gabriel and Rebecca to eggs and an occasional chicken.

Gabriel was obviously weaker than when his children had seen him last, but his will was indomitable, and patronizing remarks about his health were brushed aside to get to the matter at hand. "You are each adult and will go wherever you want and do whatever you want today, but tomorrow I want each of you here for our evening meal without fail." He disregarded all light-hearted banter spoken in response, and so his words stood with force.

The father spent much of the next day in his room in bed, another indication that he was weak. Rebecca helped him downstairs to the dining room just before the meal was to be served.

The daughters had helped prepare the chicken with artichokes in a white sauce. The bed of rice had a very small touch of saffron which is the right amount. Everything in the salad was from their garden, butter lettuce, cucumbers, tomatoes, and basil. The olive oil came from this house by way of the neighborhood olive press. The press operator insisted that each customer visit and inspect to see that the temperature of the olives was kept cold during the crushing and extraction process for the greatest retention of aroma and flavor.

Gabriel said grace. He stood and remained silent for almost a minute and then asked that the food give them the strength to fulfill the will of their Maker.

Just before the meal ended, the father spoke again. "I have brought you here tonight for a reason. I would like for your mother to tell you a story before I speak again."

The older son ignored the admonition in scripture to honor his father in his old age and ignored the commandment to honor his father and his mother. "You are going to allow a woman to speak at your table, to address us?"

"It is my command, yes."

Before beginning, Rebecca thought about the day a few years ago when their burro had quit. He was old and apparently decided he had done enough and would do no more no matter the consequences. She suddenly understood the burro's decision better tonight than she had that day. She felt tired of her older son's rigidity and ingratitude. For the sake of Gabriel, she would finish this. Besides, their second son was sweet and such a comfort.

She had never spoken of herself. Everything she said tonight was news to the four.

"I was raised in a village one day's walk from here to the east. I had a younger brother who was inseparable from the neighbor's child. Where there was one, there was always the other. They lived at both houses as if both families had two sons. One day they were playing outside and throwing rocks. The neighbor child threw a rock that struck my brother on the side of his head. He shouted for help, and my father carried my brother to the house. He died a few hours later, and the villagers held a meeting.

The burial was to take place the next day from our house. My little brother's body was there since there was no religious place of worship. The neighbor child and his parents came, even knowing what the villagers had decided. The village spokesman said, "Since the child had taken a life, he must be stoned to death."

After a long look at her older son to make a point, Rebecca continued. "Without permission, my mother spoke and said to the townspeople, 'I have lost one son and will not lose my other son. This living son will be even more welcome than before and his parents also. I cannot stop you, but anyone who wants to harm my remaining son will have to harm me first.'"

Until tonight Rebecca's children knew nothing of their mother's brother or that the "uncle" who occasionally visited them as children had accidentally killed him and been forgiven and been so loved that his life was spared.

Rebecca's story was over. Gabriel thanked her and said to his children, "That child was killed by accident, and his true friend was saved by your grandmother's love and forgiveness.

"I have been having a dream lately that is somehow connected. Whether I am hearing God's voice or God is allowing me to voice what I think He wants me to understand does not matter. I am before the Eternal Tribunal and am being asked if I have instructed my children properly.

That dream has been upsetting me. Last night the dream changed. I was being asked the same question when I was told to hold my answer since another case was interrupting mine. A young man was being asked why he was there as his ordained time had not yet come. I felt I was supposed to witness the case which interrupted mine for a reason.

"The young man replied, 'I would gladly have come later, at my appointed time, but another young man decided that I was not following Your will and put fatal holes in my body with a weapon… during my wedding.'"

Gabriel continued. "It was as if I heard His voice in my dream. 'When I invite someone at a certain time, it is wrong for someone else to change that certain time intentionally. I created time. It belongs to Me. If one person thinks someone else is not following My will, I have allotted all the time in both lives to learn My will and follow it. To force someone to follow My will defeats the purpose of creation, of choosing Me freely.'"

Gabriel stopped. His story was also complete.

The daughters were impressed with both stories but silent. The older brother still thought it was a mistake to have allowed her to speak at the table, and his cold demeanor conveyed that. The stories were powerful, however, and he did not think it wise to break the silence and the mood that surrounded them.

The two stories, however, obviously had a great impact on the younger brother. The sweet, obedient, usually compassionate son had begun to cry silently and then to actually shake and sob. He knelt before the chair of his mother and put his head down on the floor before her. He patted her sandaled feet. He spoke no words to her. Finally, he rose and knelt before his father.

"Your dream has saved me, saved my soul. It has caused me to change what I was going to do. Thank you, Father."

———•———

Gabriel knew that in the fullness of time, he would go the way of all the earth and finally appear before the Eternal Tribunal and be able to say that, yes, he had conveyed His message to his children. And he was certain that he would sleep peacefully until then.

# SARAH'S PLACE

John Robb shared a small spartan apartment with another student two blocks from the law school. They had graduated and were now studying for the July bar exam.

To get to this point, John Robb had slowly sold everything he owned except his car and furniture. He had cashed in what he had in retirement, sold his house in his hometown, then the note he had retained—the stock he had sold first. When the tuition was due during the last semester, he sold a piece of raw land to the mailman. He had flipped burgers, dug ditches, and, most recently, like most of his class, had clerked in a law office. Few of the class knew or cared that the rail in the courtroom was the bar. Passing the bar meant they could sit in the front of the courtroom past the bar. If it was not on the exam, nobody cared, at least for now.

The student in the next apartment was coming back from another kind of bar at this very early hour in the morning. He had perfect attendance at Drink 'n Drown but always managed to pass every class and graduate. His family traveled to the graduation because they did not believe it.

As this neighbor staggered and stomped his way along the second-story balcony, John's phone, a landline he shared with his roommate, began to ring.

"Who is this? Why are you calling me so early?"

"Ok, ok. Guess which of the boys from the center found a body in the desert?"

"Hmm. David."

"Ok, ok. Glasses or braces?"

"Braces, of course. David, with glasses, wouldn't go out in the desert to save his life. He might get dirty. Now, if you had asked me which of the boys had <u>put</u> a body in the desert…."

"Watch the news at 4:00. Later."

Studying for the Texas bar was tough enough. Really intense. Practicing for the multi-state where all the choices seemed equally good or equally bad stunk. Practicing for the essay section was only slightly easier now that he learned what the examiners wanted. No poetry. No literary references. Nothing clever, nothing wordy. Just the right answer if you knew it, then move on. Oh, and no Latin quotations.

"Wish I had known that three years ago."

Flashback images of a shy, charming adolescent mesmerized by crime—braces and rebellious hair—would intrude throughout the day. His suggestion for a group activity was to put smack in the soup and see what happens. He showed tolerance of the youngest group member and helped him eliminate the last remnants of his baby vocabulary. "You don't have toofies; you have teeth." Once when the group of his peers unanimously announced they hated him, he replied with a tiny, confident smile, "You can't fool me. I know you like me."

Despite a grueling day of study groups, practice tests, and formal bar review classes, he remembered he had an appointment with the news at 4:00. He no longer owned a television, so he ate a light early dinner at a nearby Luby's Cafeteria where a group of people quietly watched the news from around the state every night. David's news item was being broadcast from a station in the Odessa area. It was the first time he had seen David in about ten years since the pre-trial Diversion Juvenile Center was closed. The center was a pioneer program which was an expensive success. It was a privatized program for keeping salvageable kids out of the system. In this program, the juveniles had to answer to their group, which monitored their behavior with adult guidance. David's group had completed its program just before the center was disbanded.

———•———

"What's that noise? Hmm. Oh, the phone. Where is it? It's still dark. Who could be calling so early?"

"Hello?"

"So, anyway…what did you think of that? David on television told the murderer to turn himself in within a week, or he would find him. Telling him, he would talk to him again— on television. Said he would talk him in."

"If the murderer knew what we know, he would turn himself in, plead guilty, and ask for no visitors. David is tenacious."

"Did you recognize him?"

"Yes, but no braces and combed hair was a great disguise. Same chin, Same eyes, Same confidence."

"Is he in danger?"

"Just from the murderer and law enforcement so far. The person who discovers the body is always suspected."

"Later."

———◆———

The bar exam would start next Thursday. Throughout the state, each bar review company was wrapping up its series of presentations that had compressed law school into a few weeks of intense lectures by the best instructors in the state from rich and poor, large and small law schools.

Most of this group had attended the same school where their dean forced all students to take all courses that would be tested on the bar exam. John was grateful. Some thought it an abridgment of their rights.

Fortunately, there was no time to argue. The class was diverse, some very rich and some very poor, scraping along with very few loans and surviving on part-time clerking salaries from small law firms. When the price of macaroni and cheese was raised two cents a box by local grocers, it was the talk of one part of the class. John kept a jar of peanut butter and a spoon with him for when he was too hungry to concentrate. Others, also, had sold their furniture in anticipation of moving back to their hometowns to start a practice among friends and acquaintances. "Starve where it counts" was the advice of an older lawyer, John's informal mentor who rented space in the law firm's building. Three times he had asked John, as a favor, to research tough legal issues, including an oil and gas issue, one family law matter, and an adverse possession property problem for the attorney's practice. Within a few days,

John would find that each miraculously was on the exam's essay section. Plus, the old attorney had paid John for all his research just before John left the firm to prepare for the bar. That was wonderful.

The owner of one of the law review companies was standing on the stage of a packed amphitheater making the final presentation himself to this very motivated group. The presenter was fat and flamboyant and had wide red suspenders. His goal today was to reassure his audience with humor, encouragement, and very solid advice.

"Ignore anyone who says you chose the wrong review course— you and I know better. Next week you will prove it.

"If the person next to you throws up, ignore it and any accompanying odor. Someone will come and clean it up.

"This is not a good time to change your major personal habits. Don't break up with anyone, and try not to get dumped. If you are on prescription medication or possibly non-prescription medication, you might wait until after the bar exam to make any changes.

"As I told you in my first session when you return home, your old friends will know if you did not pass the bar and will be most sympathetic and say, 'Poor guy' or 'You'll do better next time.' And when you walk away, they will all say something different.

"If you know the answer, put it down succinctly and move on. Pace yourself. There will be areas where you need to spend more time thinking and organizing. Scan the entire section very quickly and then scan each separate question for issues. Organize, then answer.

"Study until it is time to stop. If you have been listening to your grandfather here, studying hard, attending the presentations, reviewing, you will know when it is time to stop studying and relax. After a night's rest, you will be fresh and calm, and all three years of law school and these review sessions will stay in order in your mind, ready to be summoned at your command. If you study at the last minute or listen to jabbering, you will jumble everything together, panic, and confuse yourself.

That is almost all.

"Mr. John Robb, some gentlemen would like to speak to you," indicating two "suits" near the podium, looking grim.

A voice from the departing crowd, "Does he need a lawyer? He could wait until the grades come out." There was no reaction by the suits, but there was a great amount of laughter at this remark. Spontaneity and wit were highly valued in law school, but the presenter's eyes looked a little fearful and sad for the only time during his upbeat session. He dismissed himself.

"Are you Mr. John Robb?"

"You must know that I am. How can I help you?"

"Even if you pass the bar exam, there is still a background check you must pass before you can be sworn in. A charge of impeding a state murder investigation would slow you down quite a bit."

Instantly he thought, "Care plan. In fact, care plans." As a former director of a center where psychologists and psychiatrists staffed every child, he got pretty good at sizing people up and deciding on an individualized plan like the doctors would normally devise. It helped him deal with difficult people, whether children or adults.

"This hasn't gone very well so far. Let's start over. I am John Robb. If I can help you, I will."

He studied both men quickly and carefully, made some decisions, and then extended his hand to the detective he suspected was in charge and gave orders and shook his hand. The lead detective had not said one word. The subordinate who had threatened him would not shake his extended hand but spoke again. "We expect your cooperation regarding a murder suspect, David Santana. We know so far that you were the director of the center which he attended. We don't have his juvie record yet, but we know you have been in contact with him."

Ignoring the rude subordinate altogether, he studied the silent partner intensely and addressed only him. "If you leave him alone, he will convince the killer to turn himself in, or he will identify him. I have not seen him or spoken to him in ten years, certainly not recently. You probably know that. I know you are allowed to mislead people, but people who lie to you can be charged.

"If I speak to you again, it would be helpful for you not to make obviously false statements, not to try to intimidate me by embarrassing me in front of my law class, and not to threaten me. You will never find a person, even a detective, with more fervor for justice and more reverence for life than the young man you are falsely accusing of murder. When I worked with him, he loved crime-solving. He believes in seeking justice in his unorthodox way. Goodbye."

Leaving the lecture hall, he wondered about the intentional misstatements and even more about the intense animosity.

One phone call by the detectives would have revealed David's participation in the center's program and John Robb's name as director, but why the strong push to pin a murder on David?

———•———

The young man accused by the detectives was ordered by his company not to wear his uniform with the company logo on television and not to mention where he worked or how he found the body at a recently closed down drilling tower that was about to be moved. As if he needed to be told not to wear a uniform with his name tag on television. Besides, apparently, one detective had been to the company office but not the drill site for the name and whereabouts of the employee who had found the body. The specific instructions from the head office of the oil company where he worked were handed to him when he arrived at the new drill site in the middle of the desert, near Monahans, Texas.

"Do not wear your uniform on television and do not indicate where you are working. We do not care what you say, but you need to be at work on time every day we work. You can talk this guy in if you can. We do not care but do your detective work on your own damn time. One other thing. Do not get killed on the new job site."

*Everyone who thinks the company attorneys approved that,*
*raise your hand.*

He would do a second television appearance, and after that, he would only work with the radio stations. There was slightly less danger. The killer could show up at the television station and shoot him, too. Besides, the radio stations were more flexible, and it was more dramatic being invisible.

He had announced he would do a second broadcast that night at a television station in the Odessa area. He had some time off while the drilling tower was being assembled at the new site. The television station was planning an interview format. That was not going to happen. In fact, he would go to another station in the Midland/Odessa area unannounced, and he thought they would probably want to broadcast his appeal to the killer while the detectives were looking for him at the original television station.

He would shower twice and wear the Dollar Store clothes and tennis shoes he had just bought, so the odor of diesel fuel would not give away where he worked to the station employees.

He still loved solving mysteries in books, on television crime shows, and even in the newspaper. Normally, he liked to keep an open mind about how the killer could be anyone. This time he already knew who it was. He did not know who the killer was exactly, but he had seen him. He had been there when it happened. He was the last worker at the site being shut down and was waiting for his ride.

The crew began very early each morning to avoid the blistering afternoon desert heat. His crew's job was to drill down several thousand feet in an area where oil was already located. Now the oil needed pressure to continue producing. The drills had been pulled, and another crew would pump water into this hole to cause pressure on the oil to break it from the shale that held it. This rig would be moved and reassembled at the next site.

He was retrieving his lunchbox and huge water bottle from the back of the grease truck when the downpour started. The windshield, covered with red-tinted sand and diesel fuel, faced the entry road to the job site. Despite the odor of diesel fumes, he could wait here and see when his ride arrived. The rain drummed on the flat roof of the old mail truck painted yellow and faded as David watched the water saturate the large, army green mesquite bushes and smaller creosote and yellow yucca. The temporary dirt road into the site circled the vegetation.

The rain had stopped briefly, and David could barely hear the motor of a vehicle winding its way through this dirt road. He first thought it was his coworker who had promised him a ride. He moved to the front of the grease truck to honk the horn to tell his ride where he was since the sun reflected off the windshield, making the dark interior invisible but stopped when he saw a large, late model white car instead. Two men got out. They were very mismatched.

The passenger got out first and started walking past a fueling platform where the ground was saturated with diesel, heading in the general direction of the grease truck. His clothes looked tattered. The driver, wearing a suit, walked up behind him into the area saturated with diesel and shot him with a pistol in the back of the head.

When he heard the car drive away, he checked the body of a skinny young man now caked with diesel and soaked with the rain, which had resumed. The left arm was twisted behind, and he could see the needle marks. His left hand was soft, and his fingernails were neglected and dirty. Track marks and no callouses meant probably not an oil field worker. He thought the pistol had been a twenty-two, not very loud and small. Also, the dead man's hair was cut very short, and the entrance wound was easily visible and very small.

The body was face down in the wet dirt. A film of diesel floated on top of the puddles of water surrounding the dead man's head, making kaleidoscopic rainbows. He reached for a wallet in the back pocket of faded jeans. There was no wallet but an expired state-issued identification card, which he extracted by one corner. David studied it, then wiped the corner he'd touched and returned it.

He was not the most stable person on earth to start with, and this had shaken him. The dead guy was his same age according to the id card.

He began to walk away from the site in the direction of his ride and thought there was no mystery even though all footprints and tire tracks were being washed away. He saw the killer, although he did not know who he was yet. This time, this crime, all his planning was for proof. Ok, and maybe a little drama.

His short letter to each radio station included a method to verify that it was him, the same guy from the television. He was not formally religious, but the only book in his temporary hotel room was the Gideon Bible. Four radio stations. So, four different psalms for each station.

These psalms were delivered to the stations. When he called in, he would indicate the psalm he had delivered to each station for that night, and the station would know it was him.

He had four really old flip phones that could not be traced. Probably. Not to him, certainly. He had taken them from a police evidence room in a small town in Northern Mexico. They were confiscated phones destined for destruction. He had a friend who had more or less accidentally become a sheriff of the town when the sheriff died.

He had jokingly told his friend, "Follow the duct tape, and you will follow the marijuana shipments."

Invariably, bundles of pot were wrapped in plastic with massive amounts of always grey duct tape. Sure enough, his friend watched the biggest buyers of duct tape, and everyone who was not in the construction business was followed. He got the phones because his friend owed him a favor.

———•—•———

That night his coal-black eyes looked directly into the television camera of the station that had not been expecting him. "Last night, I spoke to you about the enormous pain and burden you are experiencing, the horrible pain of taking a human life whether you can admit it or not. There is no peace.

"I am not a religious person. In fact, I am probably not even a good person. I will tell you, though, that this cannot be tolerated. I will continue to encourage you to answer for taking a human life. The great burden you feel was not meant for any human to carry. You can't.

"In his own time, God takes the life of every person He has ever created. Except in self-defense or in a just battle, it is a burden I think He reserves for Himself alone. I hope to talk to you four more times to encourage you, but you must start moving toward turning yourself in. Picture yourself already past confessing and imagine the relief. I would rather have you correct this before Wednesday night.

"Oh, yeah. I almost forgot. I think it would be good if you do not kill me. Killing me will not reduce the pain and burden you are carrying. It will only increase and prolong your suffering. The killing itself may appear to have been committed by a person without remorse. Look at my face. I do not believe that.

"I will talk to you tomorrow, God willing. Good night."

———•—•———

"Did I wake you?"

"No, surprisingly enough. I am up studying. The bar is in five days. Besides, the detectives were already here this morning. They found out more about our center. They already knew that David was a participant. They heard how the Center was run, how we implemented each child's care plan, and how we kept daily, weekly and monthly notes for the next staffing.

They wanted my handwritten notes on David. They want to charge me with obstruction."

"Did you still have any notes?"

"No, they were collected and destroyed when the center was closed. The decision was made that the children were entitled to their privacy if there were no crimes involved. Now the detective claims David killed the victim at his job site over a drug deal.

"Of course, I think David already knows who it is. Remember how theatrical he was when solving little mysteries? I think he is going to draw this out, so the killer sees that his identity is obvious.

"Last night, the station said he's switching to radio and that detectives were at the station where they expected him to appear last night. I expect he has pre-recorded his statements and won't appear at any radio station."

"Would you?"

"Later."

———•———

For three nights, radio ratings throughout West Texas went through the roof. Even the television stations were announcing the times of the radio broadcasts. The local paper printed recaps of the statements on page one. The youngest editor of the smallest paper in West Texas, Madison Parker, transcribed each broadcast and repeated them all in order. She even ran special editions, an almost obsolete idea, but syndicated papers picked up her stories. One tabloid reported there were bookies in Vegas taking bets on how long David would live.

Each night that same voice urged surrender and added facts that made discovery and capture seem inevitable, at least to the listening audience.

"I am begging you to turn yourself in. Not many people would want to take the life of such a young drug addict. Was he a snitch? A blackmailer? A threat? You stood behind him in dirt soaked with diesel fuel to shoot him.

You will never get the smell out of your shoes, and tomorrow you will have to explain why you are wearing different shoes. Remember, tomorrow night, Wednesday, will be my last talk with you. Please, nothing that happens after turning yourself in will be as bad as right now. Thanks for listening."

Wednesday morning, the detectives had been at all the radio stations in the area and demanded any tapes that would be played that night. The obnoxious detective, the only one who spoke, claimed the stations were impeding a murder investigation and that statements by the murder suspect, David Santana, were evidence. Each station was ordered to announce that David was armed and dangerous.

Someone wanted him not captured but dead.

One of the station owners told the detectives that they could go directly to hell and take their search warrant with them. "That young man is not a person of interest -— he is an interesting person. He is not stupid. We do not have any tapes. He calls in each night, verifies that it is him, and then plays the recording over the phone."

When the courts were closing for the day, the suits returned to each station with a court order prohibiting the stations from broadcasting any statement by David Santana as it might contain information that would help any of his possible accomplices. The detectives would have arrested him but found the drilling operation had moved to an unknown site. It was likely that the suspect was sharing a trailer with coworkers who were not eager, just as a general rule, to attract the attention of the police.

The radio stations periodically announced that they were being prevented from broadcasting David's final statement even if he called it in. That probably raised as much interest as David's planned broadcast. The level of drama was satisfactory from David's point of view, but the level of danger was also increased.

———•———

Meanwhile, that magic moment of inner peace had arrived for John Robb, at least regarding the Texas bar exam. It was five in the afternoon, and pass or fail, he had done all that he could do and was taking the presenter's last piece of advice. He would do something different to distract himself for the evening.

Three calls brought the needed distraction. The first call was expected.

No preamble. "This is David. They are trying to blame the murder on me and kill me. One radio station is saying the detectives have asked for SWAT to execute my arrest. I called the detectives to say there was a mistake. A very angry detective told me the same thing and said they had a court order to tap your phone. I am not worried about not talking on the radio tonight. I want to live.

"Do you remember how you would take me to Sarah's Place so I could talk out my problems to her because she was so non-judgmental?"

"I remember. You called her your Middle Eastern therapist."

"That is where I went today after I talked with that detective. I came back to town again just for that. Sarah has sure lived a long time.

"I know what the killer looks like, but I do not know who he is."

"This case will be solved tonight, David. You will be safe. I will call you very shortly."

Next came the call from the difficult detective.

"Now I have proof that you are assisting a murderer. Your phone call just now was recorded. No bar exam for you, buddy, just like I said. By the way, my partner said he had already tracked down Sarah and had interviewed her at length. She filled him in on David Santana. It is as good as any confession.

"I will have the pleasure of announcing this development tonight on the radio in place of the murderer's final, phony appeal."

"Thank you for calling me, detective. You have just solved the case. I will ask David to call you and explain a most important detail you might want to know before you go on the radio."

———•———

"Detective, this is David. Please record what I am about to say."

"Don't worry about that."

"I won't. There is an alpaca farm very near here. I will give you the phone number and address which you will want to verify. At the very back of the farm is a corral. The owner took in a retired circus camel that I used to visit when I was in the juvie program and had many problems."

"Listen, idiot, is there some point here?"

"Oh, yes, sir. I visited there today. Above the corral entrance is a sign that says *Sarah's Place*. I would love to have you go on television or radio and tell how your partner interviewed Sarah. That would be enough drama even for me. There is one thing I want even more—- for you to catch the killer.

"I just can't let you go on the radio or television and say that your partner interviewed a camel."

Call number three.

"How will you be able to concentrate on the bar exam while David is in danger?"

"I think he will be very safe after tonight's broadcast. Listen to the radio at the regular time."

———•———

"Good evening. My voice is not the voice you were expecting, but this last message from David will be the same. No court has ordered me not to talk, although I am speaking with David's permission.

"A courageous young man told the murderer of another young man to find it within himself to surrender by the end of tonight's broadcast, or his identity would be revealed. Four radio stations and two television stations have agreed to allow me to announce the surrender of the murderer or his arrest thirty minutes from now. Failing his surrender, his identity will simply be announced.

"One last thing. I know you are listening. This is John Robb. I know who you are. I have shaken your hand and looked you in the face. I suggest to your obnoxious partner that he look at your shoes and then look you in the face and tell you that it is now time."

# TENNIS SHOE SALVATION

The very proper, slightly grim Mrs. Clark buttoned her not quite thick enough old, gray wool coat to combat the icy blast of wind and got on the city bus for her twenty-minute ride to her tenement apartment where she lived with two grandsons. She had just left her doctor, and most of her thoughts on the bus ride were about the repetitious report of her health. She did, however, notice that the plastic seat would only be properly warm just about when she was getting off the bus.

The exam had started and concluded the same as usual. The busy, young doctor was studying her chart and medical history. "Do you mind if I call you Susan?"

"Yes, I mind. My name is Mrs. Clark. I told you that last year.

At the conclusion of her exam, she watched him looking over the results for a while and then said, "What's wrong?"

"Now, Su…, or rather Mrs. Clark, you have led a very long and full life."

"Never mind that. I want to know what's wrong."

"Absolutely nothing, Mrs. Clark. You are obnoxiously healthy. If you stay on your blood pressure medication, we can have this same conversation again next year."

She thought about it on the bus. His attempt at humor fell flat for two reasons: he wasn't funny, and, considering the harshness of her life, the thought of death as a blessed release was comforting. Before she got to her stop, however, Mrs. Clark decided that comforting relief was off the table. She had to think of Sam, so she readjusted her thinking, returning to her usual grim, dutiful attitude. The thought of living longer might have depressed a weaker person but not Mrs. Susan Clark. Once she decided it was a matter of duty, she swept aside thoughts of dying any time soon. By the time she unlocked the door of her small, second floor, two-bedroom apartment and hung her coat and taken off her very old scarf, she was planning dinner for when the boys got out of school, mac and cheese and pork chops and a nice salad. Maybe weak tea.

Upon her retirement from full-time nursing two years ago, she had set money aside for a modest funeral and put the rest into an annuity for the boys and had allowed it to grow. They lived off her social security check and her part-time nursing jobs. The boys knew nothing of her finances.

Sam's birthday was tomorrow, one week before hers. She had saved from her income as a private duty nurse and had bought him the best tennis shoes the store had. The shoes were wrapped and ready for tomorrow. She would bake a chocolate cake in the morning, but she had a private duty shift later tomorrow and would not finish until midnight. She sat at the kitchen table and planned tomorrow night's meal. The chicken and rice with cheese would cook all afternoon on low in the crockpot and be ready for Sam and Rodney's supper just in time. She also thought about her only patient, an amazing lady, happy in the face of death, who prayed for healing not for herself but for her nurse. "When was the last time you were genuinely happy, the last time you really laughed?"

*Who could laugh? Rodney was rocking along, pleasant and sociable, but Sam...*The city had the highest homicide rate in the nation. Tempers flared over some slight, guns were abundant, and someone's son or grandson died, and the shooter went to prison forever. Realistically, she did not want to outlive Sam. Too often, his solution to the conflict was anger. Of course, he was large and strong, but that was nothing to a bullet. Anger was a magnet attracting more conflict and rage and stupid solutions.

Sam was not eligible to play basketball again until semester grades came out, which made him seethe. Meanwhile, the new captain of the team, Isaac, was not his friend. They were the same size, right down to their shoe size. Isaac had replaced Sam when the last set of grades disqualified Sam, and that made it worse. Sam would be eligible only if his grade in English improved. He had volunteered to do an extra assignment to improve his grade: "Thank You, Ma'am" by Langston Hughes, about a boy who tried to steal a lady's purse to buy a pair of shoes.

Friday morning, he opened his gift and told his grandmother, "These are beautiful. Your birthday is in seven days, and I don't have anything I can give you; I'm embarrassed." He wore the shoes to school.

As fate would have it, in the crowded lunchroom Isaac, with his size 11 shoe, accidentally stepped on Sam's brand new, size 11 white tennis shoe and left a smudge. His classmates had nothing better to do than stir up hatred and indicated that Sam had been insulted by Isaac, his competitor, and he had to do something about it at the game tonight or be disgraced.

Sam and Rodney enjoyed the slow-cooked chicken and rice and cheese dish, which had simmered all afternoon. Then they enjoyed large slices of chocolate cake. Sam then suggested that Rodney do his homework while he did the dishes. That was unusual. Rodney did his homework at the kitchen table. That was only slightly less unusual. When Sam was finished, he told Rodney, "I am going to the gym for a little while, but I won't stay."

Rodney had heard rumors at school already and asked, "Is there going to be trouble?"

With an assuring smile, Sam said, "No, I am going to do something nice for grandmother's birthday. No trouble."

He left the house with two large paper grocery bags with the tops folded down.

Friday night was the team's big game. He first made a very brief stop at the receptacle outside the police department, where he deposited one of the bags. Sam showed up at the front gate of the gym carrying the second large brown grocery bag. He went straight to the locker room.

Isaac, of course, had heard rumors, too, and when he saw Sam and the large bag, he expected Sam to pull out a gun. Instead, he pulled out his brand-new sneakers and said, "I want you to win tonight. These are from my grandmother and me. I can only stay for the team prayer."

Mrs. Susan Clark was not psychic, but she wasn't oblivious either. The tension and anger she saw in Sam before today were in her thoughts. Her patient asked her again when she had last been happy when she had last laughed. She was expecting, not to laugh, but to hear bad news about Sam.

The next morning, she asked Rodney if he had done his homework for next week. "Yes, grandmother. I did it all while Sam did the dishes." That was so out of character that it made her worry more.

There was a gift on the table with a note. "Happy Early Birthday, grandmother. I really hope you understand. Love, Sam."

At first, she did not. Why would someone gift wrap the morning newspaper?

And why rearrange the paper with the sports section first. Then she saw why and why she would need understanding. The article was headlined, "Grandmother Gives Sneakers to Team Captain." She sat so quietly that Rodney panicked and went to wake up Sam.

Sam came in and knelt beside her chair. "I was hoping you would understand. I had an old pistol, and they wanted me to shoot Isaac because he accidentally scuffed the beautiful shoes. The pistol went to the police and the shoes to Isaac. In the Bible, he was the one who was going to be sacrificed, and then, he wasn't."

She began shaking gently with quiet laughter. She hugged both the boys at the same time. "I have to work tonight, but when my patient asks me when was the last time I laughed, I will tell her all about it—what a beautiful present. I am so blessed. Thank you, Sam."

# MORGAN MANNING

She exited the highest of the ranger lookout stations in the national park and inhaled the cold, clean pine scent carried on the breeze from the trees below. She scanned the magnificent pink and grey and blue panorama of the early September dawn. She was standing in the three-hundred-foot clearance surrounding the ranger station where she lived with her parents. The clearance is devoid of all trees because the station is above the timberline. Brush and grass have been cleared for fire safety and visibility. Except for her hiking boots, Morgan Manning is dressed for school, a sundress, and a sweater for the morning. Her school shoes are in her backpack.

She begins her descent to the trailhead, two miles below by winding trails. The trailhead is the communication center and headquarters for the park. It contains the parking lot and registration office for anyone hiking or camping in the park. Morgan stops at the office and says hello to the ranger, telling him she is starting her first school day.

"I know, Morgan. You're the talk of the forest."

The ranger was not able to hike the trails as easily as he once did but was the senior ranger and in charge of delivering food and water supplies to each of the stations on horseback with the help of two pack mules. The stations were not intentionally isolated but were strategically placed to allow the greatest view of the forests below and to collectively act as an early warning system against lightning strikes or fires caused by careless campers. All the stations were in radio contact with the main office. This system enabled the rangers to watch for campers who had not registered. More importantly, in case of an emergency, a ranger could pinpoint a hiker or camper in distress and ascertain what services were needed and who could supply those services fastest.

For her entire scholastic life, she had been home-schooled by her park ranger parents. Her education was extraordinary and on par with public school students her age if perhaps a little erratic. However, during the summer she had been tested for appropriate placement in the high school two and a half miles away partially to facilitate her entry into college next year and partially to allow her to socialize with people her age. Today she will walk the last half mile to the school for registration so as to arrive fresh. She hopes to join a cross country team. Once she is on a team, she could run to the school, shower there, and still be ready for classes.

"Morgan, I have your parents' permission to give you my small piece of advice. Academically, you're ready. Today you will meet many types of people, as varied as the animals of the forest. There are predators and those who belong to the herd—some camouflage for preservation or to hunt. Observe and then follow your instincts. But there is one creature more dangerous than any other. Only the hurt or wounded animal hunts just to kill."

His forest animal analogy stayed in the back of her mind all day, but there was so much happening. The unfamiliar noise of loud bells and shuffling feet in the hallways, lockers slamming and the cacophony of voices and clattering silverware banging against metal trays in the cafeteria, announcements from loudspeakers. Then came the compression of so many people's emotions — and such language—some of it directed toward her.

After all, she was humble and modest but strikingly beautiful. One Native American student announced upon seeing her that he was changing his Indian name to Thunderstruck. He did seem dazed. Another student abdicated his membership in a gay organization as he said, "now that he had seen the competition." The sponsor was sympathetic with his coming out but not with his reversal.

The student population was a collection of many nationalities. The girls' cross-country track team mainly consisted of Native American and African American students who approached Morgan, wanting her to join their team but expecting rejection. "I'd love to join the team."

Messages were going back and forth on cell phones which supposedly no one used during school.

The girls' coach taught chemistry in the fourth period, and the boys' coach taught math last period. During roll call last period, the teacher paused while calling her name and asked to speak to Morgan in the hallway. When he said this, several girls put their heads down as if ashamed and a few of the boys made snickering noises. But not everyone.

"We're checking all student lanyards, especially the new students. I.D. is important." He reached for Morgan's lanyard held around her neck by a strap and resting at the top of her cleavage, which was modestly covered. Just as he reached for what he was really after, she slapped him so hard that only his athletic ability kept him from falling down.

"Don't touch me, buddy. Next time I will use a closed fist."

She turned and walked back into the classroom with a very nice stride and with total composure.

Despite his reputation as a pig, the teacher thought he could bluff his way in front of the class and act as if nothing had happened. He did not know he had Morgan's perfect handprint across the entire left side of his face. The cell phones, which no one had or used, especially during class, had captured nice shots of his face and Morgan looking perfectly serene.

Morgan raised her hand. The math teacher/coach nodded to her. She walked in silence to the front of the classroom in her pale-yellow sundress." My name is Morgan Manning. Because I am new here, the coach asked me to participate in a demonstration, and I did, but may have gotten a little carried away."

The coach took over. "I want to explain to you this little demonstration. When a girl says 'No,' it means 'No.' If a person is underage, 'Yes' and 'No' both mean 'No.' No one can touch another person without permission — that is simple assault. Thank you, Morgan."

Morgan had the class's total attention. "I will demonstrate." When she was re-entering the classroom, her eyes had locked on the eyes of a very handsome young man with hatred in his eyes and rage in his heart. She recalled the ranger's advice from this morning. The wild animal in pain kills for the sake of killing.

*"Thank you, Ranger Gerard.* "She walked to the desk of the handsome one and said, "May I?"

One nod. She put her hand gently on his shoulder, nothing else. He felt the heat of her hand through his shirt, which he was pretty sure was on fire. He was sure his shoulder was branded.

That evening at the supper table in the home of Thunderstruck, "Mom, we have a new student at school named Morgan."

"Son, is Morgan a boy or a girl?"

"A girl, Mom. Definitely a girl." This mother studied her adolescent son and made a mental note.

In another household, "Mom, Dad, do you remember last year when I told you some girls complained about a coach touching them, and nobody did anything about it?"

Hesitatingly, "Yes."

"He took the new girl into the hall and came back with her handprint across the left side of his face. He explained to the class that it had been a demonstration."

But in one dysfunctional household, the student who had locked eyes with her was now conflicted. He had originally made up his mind to select a target worthy of their mutual degradation and socially destroy that person. When he first saw her, he decided here was a person worthy of his efforts and worthy of their combined social destruction. The product of being raised or ignored by a drunken, abusive stepfather and a weak, non-protective mother, he was handsome, smart, athletic, and bitter. But that touch brought him nothing but confusion.

The first part of his original plan was to make her love him, but it was odd how she spotted him and locked eyes, and chose him from the whole class for her demonstration. Her touch was peaceful, burning and peaceful at the same time. He would gather more information about her and not solidify any plans yet.

The next day their first class together was third period. English. He was very good at manipulation. He had a non-verbal agreement with his parents to leave him alone in exchange for a reduced amount of hatred toward them. He would try his silent treatment and menacing look on her again, but she was light years ahead of him.

Without preamble, with her eyes looking into him, "Yes, I will go to the prom with you if you haven't killed me by then. What is your name? I mean, I wouldn't want to go with the wrong young man accidentally."

His eyes smoldered. He could not stare at her enough. Or even talk.

"You are invited to supper tonight with my parents. We can meet at the park trailhead at five. Ok?"

He smoldered and fumed but nodded.

After school, Morgan stopped for a visit with Ranger Gerard. "So, how was your second day of school?"

"Mixed. I have some great teachers, one pervert. Also, a lot of amazing students, some want me on their cross-country team."

"What are we leaving out?"

"I was saving it for last—the wounded one. A boy looked at me with fire in his eyes. Naturally, he's coming to supper. Yesterday you told me to trust my instincts, and I always have. I know he wants me damaged, partly, but partly he wants to love me and not hate himself. Would you mind if I invite him to help me deliver the supplies to the stations this weekend?"

"Good idea, but be careful. I want to meet him first."

"Perfect. He will be here at five. May we ride the horses to my parents'?"

"Well, they do need the exercise, so it is a good use of government property."

"Thanks, ranger."

That evening they tied the horses in a shed at the back of her parents' station. When they entered, the smell of eggplant parmesan and garlic bread filled the spartan living room.

"Mom, this is Aldo."

"I am very happy to meet you, Aldo."

Her father heard her voice and had just come into the room. To him, she said, "Dad, this is Aldo. I have offered to marry him, but he is conflicted between marriage and murder."

To have his deep, smoldering emotions recognized and announced so flippantly paralyzed him for a moment.

"Well, son, I think marriage and murder have a lot in common."

"Just what do you mean by that, dear?"

"Let's see you get out of this one, Dad."

"Well, dear. Take two giant pine trees. One you burn completely. The other you allow to rot and decay until it is completely decomposed. Which puts off more heat?"

Aldo spoke. "They put off the exact same amount."

"That's right. It's the same with passion. Pace yourself. I would suggest saving some of the heat for old age."

His back was turned to his wife. She said, "Great save."

He rolled his eyes.

She said, "You're rolling your eyes, aren't you?"

The father said, "Wow, she's good."

After supper, Morgan offered to ride with him back down to the ranger station, but Aldo said he would lead her horse back or have her return it on her way to school in the morning. "Besides, I have a lot to think about."

———•———

The next morning, the superintendent of the school district, the coach's uncle from the earlier demonstration, happened to be in the hallway and met her. "Am I right? You are Morgan Manning, the new student. I am very happy to meet you. We are both brand new here. If you have any problems, I will listen and help you solve them."

Then at her locker, a football player, a running back, spoke to Morgan. "My name is Ivan. I would like to know if you would be willing to go out with me?"

"It is very nice of you to ask me. I am flattered, but I am already completely committed to Aldo."

"I am not trying to be mean, but he has issues. It will take years to resolve them." "I know. I am really looking forward to it."

The player laughed. "I wish you the best of luck. If you allow, I will be a friend to both of you."

# THE PARKER GIRL

Madison Parker stood at the window of the top floor of the courthouse and surveyed the small park that led to the entrance. She stood mostly on the balls of her feet, bobbing and weaving ever so slightly, unconsciously clenching and unclenching her fists. She scanned her entire view with flicks of her head, her short, straight, brown hair following.

Someone seeing her might guess this seventeen-year-old was a boxer. That would be right. Someone might think she was combative. That would be utterly wrong outside the ring.

She was wearing grey warm-up pants and a grey sweatshirt. Her high-top tennis shoes were brand new and had taken most of the money she had, which was not much. Her parents said she could not wear her old pair to court. They had holes in the sides and the bottoms.

She took what money she had to the shoe store, where the teenage clerk measured her foot. He said, "Wow," which earned a sudden look from Madison, which made him think his life was in danger for some reason.

"The reason I said 'Wow' is that we have some shoes your size on sale. He figured he was going to die anyway, so he might as well tell her. "They are an excellent brand but have not sold because they are lime green."

"But they're good?"

"Top of the line, I would not kid you. *Especially since you know where the store is.'*

Bobbing from side to side in her brand-new high-top lime green tennis shoes, she watched through the window as the bitter autumn wind scattered the multi-colored leaves all over the park and blew them against the legs of an old man sitting on a bench in an insufficient overcoat. She had passed him thirty minutes earlier on her way in and had thought his ring strategy was good. He would not miss the person he apparently wanted to see.

She knew him but did not know it. She had a part-time job selling newspapers in this building for a man she knew only by name. After school, as instructed in writing, she would take the remaining newspapers from the vending machines and sell them at a discount since many courthouse workers had computers and stayed current all day. There were still movies, obituaries, crossword puzzles, and comic strips to entice them. Also, the editor was old-style. He owned the small paper and said it like it was, which was great for the workers, although some were careful about not being seen buying the paper.

Her thoughts were mostly on her next fight in an arena where she had never been. She stood accused of stealing newspapers from the vending machines. The judge who engineered the charges was repeatedly accused of criminal behavior in the newspaper she sold. He wanted to get rid of the newspaper or at least smear its sales representative. She had actually done the research for a few of the articles, and they were accurate.

She was due for her pre-trial at 9:00 a.m. She would be alone. Her parents loved her, but they both had to work. Things were really tight. She knew they loved her and how tight things were. She gave them everything she made. Even the small amounts she made writing articles for "her" newspaper went to them when the checks came in the mail, often with instructions about pertinent subjects which might need to be developed.

"Always arrive early" was good ring advice and good advice almost everywhere. She wanted to be in the courtroom by 8:30. She asked for directions twice and received the directions along with looks that said, "You're doomed."

One last look at the park, and she would head to her fate. *'Interesting.'* She saw a man approaching the bench of the man with the inadequate overcoat. The man approaching looked athletic, "squared away, "her dad would say. The athlete and the occupant of the bench spoke, and the athlete apparently convinced the old man to trade his coat for a nice camel-colored overcoat and gloves. The old man nodded his gratitude but was still agitated. He was pointing at the courthouse, and it looked like he was pointing at her. He gave the younger man a newspaper, pointing at something within. Then the old man sat back down, and the "squared away" man disappeared from sight as he got close to the courthouse's front door.

Madison opened one of the double doors of the courtroom. One of her assignments from "her" newspaper was to write an article about the architecture of this building. It was art deco, like the old theatre near the gym where she worked out when she finished selling papers here after school. She loved the earth tones and the geometric shapes of the fixtures.

"*Wow, he's fast.*" She had only come down three flights of stairs and located her courtroom, and the squared-away man was already at a table in the front of the room, apparently asleep with his legs stretched out under the table. The sign on the table said Defense, so she sat next to him and waited.

Finally, she tapped him on the arm. "It's 9:00, time for my hearing. Could you be my attorney?"

"Are you Ms. Madison Parker?" "Yes, I am."

"Do you want me to be your attorney?"

"Yes, I do."

"Then I am your attorney. My name is Don Haig. Why did you choose me?"

"Because you gave your coat to the old man, and I think you are a fighter, a boxer."

"Why do you think that?"

"You are in shape and you rest like I do in the corner between rounds. But I don't sleep."

He nodded and looked at her face. "Use your left ten times for every right."

"My right is my strength."

"The right side of your face is getting hit too much while you are trying to use your right."

"O.K. Any other advice?"

"Yes, Get out of the ring. It's for people who need it. You have journalism scholarships available that you don't even know about."

"Any advice about today?"

"No. You will win. It will actually be an adventure. Now I have to prepare for victory."

He began to read the newspaper that the old man had given him earlier. The judge swept in and threw papers on his bench, possibly for dramatic effect.

"Who do you think you are taking a nap at counsel table, wearing a clown's overcoat, reading a newspaper in my courtroom?" Madison thought, *"They were right. I'm doomed."*

Meanwhile, Attorney Haig stood and addressed the court as if he had been politely greeted. "Good morning, your honor," a small pleasant smile on his face.

"What are you doing in my courtroom?"

Still smiling, "I have two pieces of business with this court. First, I am here to dispose of any charges against my client, Ms. Madison Parker."

"The D.A., who has just walked in, has a line of witnesses who will say they saw your little client remove entire bundles of newspapers from the machines and proceed to sell them."

"My client will stipulate (turning to Madison) that she took the newspapers from the stands without paying for them and sold them."

Tugging on the offensive coat, she whispered, "Am I going to jail?"

"Worse. School. In time for lunch. Pay close attention and take notes. This is a newsworthy story."

The district attorney asked, "Your honor, may everyone be seated?" The judge made a brushing-off motion with his hand, the rudest way he could think of to say yes.

"Are you prepared to offer a plea to this little defendant?" That earned a glance from the "little defendant."

"Yes, your honor. We were set for a pre-trial only but can have plea papers prepared immediately."

"Are you prepared to go to trial today if I reject your plea offer, Mr. District Attorney?"

"Yes, judge. All my witnesses work in the courthouse and are available."

The judge indicated to the court reporter to stop recording, always a bad sign and always illegal. "Who the hell are you, anyway?"

"I am an attorney licensed in this state. My name is Don Haig. I believe the district attorney can vouch for the fact that I am a practicing attorney."

"Well, I've never heard of you. I find it very interesting that after spotting you walking toward the courthouse in a tan overcoat, the sheriff and his deputies attempted to discover for courthouse security how you arrived in this fair city. There is no out-of-town vehicle registered at any local hotel or in our public parking. No buses or trains have arrived recently. Now you come into court in a completely different coat as if trying to disguise yourself."

"On behalf of my client, we reject any plea offer. Ms. Parker pleads not guilty."

"What! You stipulated that your little client stole newspapers, and now you plead not guilty. Sounds like contemptuous pleadings to me."

"My client stipulates that she took the newspapers from the machines every workday for the past month with the consent of the owner. We stipulate venue, jurisdiction, identification, and the act but will not stipulate that it was without permission."

The D.A. rose. "Judge, the state calls the courthouse administrator who is now here in the courtroom."

"You have been sworn in. State your name."

"Andrew Oliver.'

"Cutting right to the chase, with the consent of the court and defense attorney, you are the courthouse administrator in charge of all food and newspaper vending machines and of the contents thereof for sale, correct?

"Yes."

"Did you ever give effective consent on behalf of the newspaper corporation to this person, Madison Parker, to remove papers from the machines and sell them without paying for them?"

"No."

"Did you actually see her do that?"

"Yes, many times during this last month."

"Pass the witness."

"Do you have a written document making you the agent of the newspaper corporation?"

"I have a longstanding understanding through the county commissioners that items brought into this building will be under my supervision, care and protection. I am, therefore, the effective owner of the newspapers."

"Anything else, counselor?"

"Yes, your honor. If the actual owner of the newspaper corporation came into this building and took papers from his newspaper machines, you would not say you had a superior right to the papers, would you?"

An unpleasant smirk appeared on the face of the witness. "The newspaper owner has been banned from entering this building by a criminal trespass order of this court. His clothes, including the shabby overcoat you are now wearing, smell, and some of the workers in the building complained."

"But to answer my question, the owner of the newspaper still has a superior right to remove newspapers with or without consent, correct?"

"Yes."

"So, if the newspaper owner himself or herself removed the papers, you as the agent of the corporation could not say that the owner needed your consent, correct?

"No, but that has not happened."

"I believe this case is over." The judge was grinning.

"Your honor, I am handing the building administrator a newspaper I just borrowed from the district attorney's desk. Do you recognize it?"

"Yes, it has my stamp on it identifying it as a sample of the many papers stolen by your client."

"Perfect. Please turn to page two of the paper in your hand."

"I am not a lawyer but have heard it said in court that a newspaper contains the rankest form of hearsay and is not admissible."

The judge nodded as if he could not have said it better himself.

"I direct your attention not to an article but to the standard statement of incorporation and location, including contact information. Do you see that?"

"Yes. It states all that and then a statement about the power of a free press."

The D.A. rose. "Your honor, relevance?

"Any response before I sustain the overdue objection?

"One last question will be my best response. Courthouse administrator, who does the newspaper you are holding name as its owner? ... I am sorry, sir; you seem to be mumbling. Please read that part in a loud voice."

"Madison Parker. It continues, 'On this day, as the owner of this newspaper corporation, I give devise, and bequeath to Ms. Madison Parker, with her parents' consent, my entire newspaper corporation including all assets, machinery, real estate, all stock and the legal right to make any decisions in regard to this paper. It is my hope that she enters a new arena, that of journalism and strikes hard, just blows for truth and for freedom of the press. I offer to remain on in any capacity Ms. Parker deems fitting. I do this because newspapers are losing their financial profitability but can still be tools for great change.'"

"Your honor, the State moves to dismiss all charges."

"Not so fast. This evidence is hearsay and inadmissible."

"If the State rests, I call the former owner of the Sun Newspaper Corporation, Mr. Lawrence Clark. The court will note he has been escorted into this building and courtroom by a State Department of Public Safety officer."

"Did you write this, conveying the paper to my client?"

"Yes, after she did a journalism internship this summer for the paper, although we have never met.

"I instructed her by mail to remove the newspapers from the machines each day for two reasons: so that she would receive the deed of real property as is required and to teach her that normally, not today certainly, newspapers are most valuable when first printed."

"Has the district attorney prepared the motion to dismiss?"

"Yes, Mr. Haig, the D.A. has."

"Will you please present it to the court?"

"You seem to think you are running my court. I am signing the order dismissing the case against Ms. Parker. Next, I will be signing an order of contempt for you, and I am ordering you confined for three days."

"Thank you for this dismissal order, Judge. I have one further request before being jailed."

"Go ahead. You have one minute."

"Mr. Clark, your coat looks very nice."

"Thank you. It is very warm, too."

"Good. Please reach into your overcoat pocket and hand me the document that I hope is still there."

"Yes, here it is."

"Thank you. This is my second piece of business with this court. I will fill in the time, 9:20 a.m., and read it out loud, and then I will hand it to the judge to whom it is addressed. 'You are hereby ordered to cease and desist from all judicial activity until such time as you appear and answer charges against you before the tribunal of the Judicial Ethics Commission. Signed by the Chief Justice of the State Supreme Court.' It is effective from the time I have been authorized to fill in. I could have done this first, but it was important to deal with Ms. Parker's case first so she could get to lunch.

"Since the court has no further authority, I will dismiss myself and suggest everyone else do the same."

# DAVID DAVID

The home of Ms. Reba Washington was as quiet as it was neat. Linoleum polished, furniture waxed, the couch covered with a freshly laundered covering. Even the child asleep for the night on the couch was freshly bathed. The next house was more than a block away and belonged to a young man who never called attention to his house. No one said what he did for a living, but the word was that somewhere his mother was crying and praying. The small dress clothes of the child asleep on Ms. Washington's living room couch were on a hanger on the knob of the front door. His white shirt was ironed and his shoes were polished. The front door was open to admit a small breeze, making the room the coolest in the house. The steel screen door was locked from the inside with a slap lock that could open with a twist.

Sometime in the night, the child heard a woman screaming. He had the run of the neighborhood, and it seemed natural to his five-year-old mind to go see. He put on his play clothes and tennis shoes and went out. A large car from outside the neighborhood was parked on the street past the house of the young man whose mother was probably crying and praying. His house was dark, but the next house had all the lights on and was the source of the screaming.

A tall stranger had dragged a young woman out of the house and onto the porch and was apparently going to force her into his car. As he turned with her toward his car, he knocked the child almost off the porch. The child did not know the girl but tried to get the man to leave her alone by tugging at his arm. The man took the child's arm and twisted it until he was satisfied. It was a green break. Worse than just broken- it was splintered. The child landed at the edge of the porch and was moved out of the way by the stranger kicking him in the face, in his eye. The back of his head struck the porch pillar. The child thought he had just blinked, but when he looked again, the stranger, the car, and the girl were gone.

The child was in great pain but could not cry. He slowly started back to Ms. Reba's house, but it seemed too far. He was at the house of the son of the crying, praying mother, and tried to knock on the steel-framed screen door, but even he could barely hear the sound he made with his remaining fist. He got a rock from the front yard and climbed the three stairs to the porch again. He sat under the small metal mailbox attached to the clapboard siding and used his good left hand to bang on the iron part of the screen door.

It took a long time before the door was answered. The young man was furious. He could see no one. He slammed the front door, and the child started banging with the rock again, only more weakly. This time the front door opened, and then the screen door was unlocked and opened. The young man said, "This is going to stop."

By now, the child's eye and the entire area around his eye were swelling. His broken arm was resting in his lap and was also swollen and twisted unnaturally.

The young man was very big and had until now been very angry and using words the child had never heard before, but the child was not afraid of him. He closed his good eye briefly. When he opened it, the young man had already locked the house, brought a car from his garage, and parked in front with the motor running and the passenger door open. The young man was very tall and strong and picked the child up gently as if he weighed nothing. The child's eye continued to swell, but the imprint of a shoe's heel just above his cheekbone could be seen for now.

"This is great. Do you have any idea what will happen at the hospital when a guy with dreadlocks carries in a little crumpled cracker?"

The child would not release the dreadlock owner's thumb until the doctor heard the child say, "You saved me." The doctor pried loose the child's good hand and prepared to send the child to the orthopedic surgeon for children where the spiral fracture would be dealt with.

The doctor told the tall man the child must have had his head against something solid when he was kicked because he also had a mild concussion. The child made a small snorting noise and whispered, "Mild."

———•———

"This is the executive assistant for Mr. Tommy Martin. Please hold."

"Very funny, Tommy. What's up?"

"Well, your name came up at my salon today. Dirt, buddy."

"That's impossible. You know I'm a saint."

"Oh, yeah. I forgot. The chief's wife was in for her regular Monday appointment. She was under the hairdryer, also known as my sodium pentothal machine, and told one of her friends that a detective with a double name was being sent by the mayor's office to join the cold case section the chief just created. The chief doesn't want anybody else on his hand-picked team, especially anybody sent by the mayor. The chief heard you have a smart mouth and a terrible temper. He plans on provoking you into losing your temper and firing you at the end of your interview."

"Yikes, I need this job. Thanks, Tommy. See you at church."

"Right."

Fortunately for David David, the mayor's sister-in-law also knew more than she should have and had quite a bit to say during a funeral she attended on Tuesday with Mrs. O'Toole, a good listener. Mrs. O'Toole drove to the cemetery, and the recently deceased was all but forgotten while her passenger told her how the mayor really disliked the chief and really needed a reason to fire him and disband the newly created cold case squad. The mayor's view was that the police force was overweight with old-timers, and the chief was surrounding himself with his most loyal detectives who should all retire and make room for the mayor's men. The best part was that he had chosen a young expendable detective and pretended he wanted him on the chief's new squad. The mayor had the chief's office bugged and knew the chief would react badly and give the mayor good cause to fire the chief.

On Wednesday afternoon, the phone rang at the home of Mrs. Beulah Lee.

"Hello."

"Is your ornery grandmother home?"

"Maybe you have the wrong number."

"You know that I don't, David David."

Holding the phone away, "Grandmother, I think Mrs. O'Toole would like to talk to you." The contents of that conversation were conveyed to Mrs. Beulah Lee's grandson.

David David's interview/termination with the chief was set for 9: 00 Friday morning. He was in the unfamiliar squad room outside the chief's office one hour early to survey the battlefield. The cold case squad had five detectives present and accounted for, probably to hear the chief demolish the new guy. His door stayed open during anything controversial so he would have witnesses.

Since no one offered him a desk, he sat in one of the uncomfortable plastic chairs for visitors beside the squad room door, working quietly on his electronic tablet. Occasionally he would jot things on his paper tablet as well. He ignored stares and cheap shots for about ten minutes. Then he said to his tablet, "Google, spell Scylla and Charybdis?"

The oldest detective, the squad leader, named Johns asked, "Are those some of your suspects?"

"No, sir. Odysseus met them on his return home from the Trojan Wars. Scylla was a monster that devoured six sailors at a time when a ship got too close to the Italian shore trying to avoid the roaring whirlpool Charybdis on the Sicilian shore. My grandfather used to tell me bedtime stories from *The Iliad* and *The Odyssey*."

The only female detective asked, "What does that have to do with anything?"

"For the moment, there are six of us." The index finger at the end of his once very broken right arm circled the room. "The mayor sent me here to get me fired by the chief to have a reason to fire the chief and dissolve the cold case squad, which he has indicated could barely handle a cold case of Budweiser. His words."

The youngest of the five, known as the chief's investigeezers, asked, "So what is the roaring whirlpool?"

Almost in answer to that question, a booming voice came from the open door of the chief's office. "When that temporary new guy gets here, send him in. Might as well get it over with early."

He was a little surprised by the young detective's instant appearance in his doorway. He recovered quickly, organized his thoughts, and began slowly.

"I have seen some of your reports from other precincts, and I do not appreciate smart remarks that appear in them. Referring to someone unmarried but close to a victim as 'next of skin' or unmarried couples as 'newlybeds' or lumping a group of tips you received as a 'unanimous tip.'"

The chief got no response and decided to escalate.

"I don't like your flyer for a conference at the jail with 'breakout sessions in the afternoon.'"

Again, silence.

"I am looking at your personnel file. Is this false information, or are you actually named David David Lambchild? What kind of idiots gives their child the same first and middle name?"

"When I was adopted, both my grandfather and great grandfather were named David, and each wanted a guarantee I was named after him. My grandmother guaranteed it."

"You are a brand-new detective with absolutely no experience in solving cold cases. I want to get to your last name, but first, tell me why I should not fire you and throw you out of here."

David had not even been invited to sit but leaned over the chief's desk and spoke in a voice that did not carry into the squad room, "I have just now written down three things I invite you to consider before making a decision." He tore off the top sheet of his writing tablet and handed the chief a page with four items on it, not three.

1.  The mayor has bugged this office. He plans on allowing you to fire me and then use your abusive remarks to fire you and dissolve the squad.
2.  I guarantee I can solve one cold case by the end of next week with the very experienced detectives outside.
3.  If you reject this offer, I will be happy to explain what I think of your remarks about my grandmother, a fiercely loyal friend of yours. They would justify my termination.
4.  I am immature for now, but I, too, am fiercely loyal to you, and I want to be a cold case detective for you, even if briefly.

There was dead silence both in the chief's office and in the eavesdropping squad room for half a minute. Then the chief returned to his battlefield voice. While tearing the handwritten note first into long thin strips, the chief said, "I want some of the old murders of this city cleared up within six months, and then the members of this squad will retire or return to open cases.

"I attempted to provoke you and expected you to explode and then be fired because I do not need a loose cannon on this squad. That did not happen. Six is too many detectives, so I will place you with this squad on a trial basis and loan you out for active cases as well. I have considered the three points of your synopsis," as he held up four fingers, "and am impressed. I am returning it to you. Offer information on any cold case you have to the squad leader, Ed Johns, and I will order that you be allowed to participate."

The chief poured the now tiny pieces of the synopsis into the detective's hand and hoped the mayor's surveillance did not include video.

The chief had stopped talking, so David David returned to his guest chair near the door to the squad room.

The chief closed his office door from the outside, locked it, and worked in the squad room the rest of the morning. He did not speak except to answer his transferred calls.

His office and the office of all elected officials, and the grand jury room were swept for bugs every Monday. Everyone knew about these sweeps. The mayor knew and knew he had to retrieve his surveillance equipment from the chief's office soon. The chief knew that and planned on setting up surveillance cameras in the squad room to discover who would retrieve the equipment for the mayor. David David knew the mayor would retrieve his equipment and knew the chief would record who was sent. He knew one more thing that the chief needed to know, which could also be grounds for his termination. Before lunch would be best.

Meanwhile, the newest detective still had a job, at least for now, because of a loyal neighborhood network, because of good preparation, and because the chief was smart. He had found out everything he could about the chief. He sat for several hours in the same uncomfortable guest chair and continued working on the electronic tablet balanced on his lap inputting information regarding the cold case he had mentioned. He was also supplementing his crash course on the personality of his new boss, Chief Greg Elgin.

Stealing an occasional glance at the chief, David David saw a man in his mid-fifties who looked very fit. His hair was short but not too short to display a touch of grey.

He wore the uniform of a patrolman, no suit or dress uniform for him. The detective knew from doing his homework that the chief's men and women were most loyal to him, that he saw himself as a keeper of the peace, not a social worker. He expected excellence every day, everywhere. The police force reflected the ethnicity of the city. Sexual harassment was never tolerated, nobody played the race card, and no one had ever seen the chief laugh. The saying was that the chief's fuse was so short, there was an open flame prohibition in his presence. David David has seen him once before.

David David went back in his mind twenty years when his only name was Lambchild. He was behind a curtain in the house of one of his many aunts. The fronts of his tiny shoes were visible to then Patrolman Elgin since they were sticking out under the curtain, but the patrolman had no search warrant. The fronts of the shoes were in plain sight, but his inquiry was of an abandoned White child living among the poorest Black families of the city. He favored no one but was pragmatic. He observed the fronts of the shoes were really shined. He made his decision. His report would reflect that the story about the abandoned White child living at various houses in the south side was unsubstantiated, perhaps another urban myth like the alligators. When his grandmother eventually learned of this, she became a fierce lifetime fan of Patrolman Elgin.

His men were working a little more quietly than usual, absorbing the fact that the temporary new guy was not fired and that the chief's office was radioactive for some reason.

Just before noon, the chief stood and said, "I want a quick meeting with you six at four. Dismissed."

Detective Lambchild saw the room empty quickly and approached the chief silently with another note. "I left my bible in the mayor's office. I want to retrieve it, and I want you to know I am going there only for that purpose."

The chief sat back down and wrote his own note. "You work for me. If you are reporting back to the mayor, you do not work for me."

One more note from the detective, "I left it there for my protection. I must retrieve my bible before Monday."

The chief unlocked his office and gestured for David David to enter. Aloud, the chief said, "In the event you happen to see the mayor, you might thank him for his confidence in you for recommending you for the cold case squad."

"Yes, sir."

"I understand you have been summoned to a district court this afternoon. You have received time off from your squad leader, Ed Johns, but will owe two hours to make up for the time you are out."

"Dismissed."

Before going to lunch, the chief gave some thought to a mayor who had the nerve to bug his office and to his new employee who had the nerve to bug the mayor's office somehow using a Bible and letting him know without actually telling him about it.

Among David David's many community contacts was a retired criminal family named Pigeon. The son was out of town once again on government business, a euphemism for being in prison or, in this case, state jail. The retired Pigeon contacted David David because he had inherited his grandson while his son was away, and the child had quit talking. David David had known the son and grandfather for more than ten years and the grandson for his entire life of three years.

The grandchild's reaction was not surprising. He had moved more times than Lewis and Clark and had lived with many different people. And he missed his father.

"Almost the only thing he says is, 'Bye, David David,' and that is five minutes after you leave. He keeps his chin on his chest and is sad and depressed most of the time. And he glares."

The newest cold case detective knew the statistics for children of prisoners and knew those who did not follow their parents were blessed with interventions by concerned people. He visited often and noticed three-year-old Samuel was acting out by hitting and pushing him, partly playing and partly angry. David David's response was always the same, "Don't push me, buddy."

Pigeon Junior, Samuel's father, was being brought back to the judge and court where he had been sentenced. Today the judge would decide whether his shock probation of six months had been completed satisfactorily and whether he could complete his time with community supervision.

So far, present in the courtroom were Pigeon Senior with his grandson, the court reporter, and David David, who was given permission by the chief and his squad leader to attend. The judge swept in exactly on time and asked where his bailiff was and where the prisoner was. The bailiff entered and expected trouble.

Normally, the judge liked to take time out to annoy his staff for any transgression such as tardiness, but he had other things in mind after the bailiff announced that the prisoner was being brought in by the transport officers from the state jail and would arrive shortly.

Samuel was standing in the open area before the bench when the judge came in. The judge decided Samuel was someone he could intimidate while he waited and locked eyes with the child. Samuel put his chin on his chest and froze in place. The judge had first taken the bench but had descended and was now also before his bench. With almost no thought, he pushed Samuel toward his grandfather.

The three-year-old's response born of a lifetime of frustration would have made any rattlesnake on the planet proud. "Don't push me, buddy." He now faced the judge and was more than ready. His small fists were clenched.

The judge's initial reaction was to do again exactly what the child forbid. Suddenly, the detective stood between the judge and the child. "May I?" Without waiting for a response, he sat right on the courtroom floor in the open area facing Samuel, now eye level with him. "Samuel, the judge wants you to sit with your grandfather until your father gets here." Without rising, he spoke softly to the judge but still faced Samuel, who was taking his ever-loving, angry sweet time about returning to his grandfather. "My name is Detective David David Lambchild. I am a friend of this family, including Samuel here. I am sure we do not need a record of what has just happened. From a child's point of view, he was pushed. I might add he just spoke his first complete sentence, rather clearly, I thought.

"I understand you will decide right now whether this child's father will be released to complete his sentence on probation while residing at home or will be sent back to the state jail. This child will demand more from him than any probation officer. I hope you don't mind my input." He rose and returned to his place beside the Senior Pigeon.

Almost without exception, people who serve as district judges are intelligent. The judge assumed his bench taking the route that kept him furthest from the child. The judge asked the bailiff to accompany the prisoner when he arrived and remove any shackles or handcuffs before bringing him in, and while waiting, he thought about the law of simple assault. "The accused knows or should know the contact would be considered offensive...."

With a nod toward the court reporter, the judge called the case, indicating that the defendant was present and could remain seated since he now had his son on his lap with the court's approval. The judge recited that he had received the probation department's recommendations and received input from law enforcement and from one relative, this with a wary glance at the child.

"You, sir, are granted community supervision for the rest of your sentence unless you violate your probation or unless I dismiss it earlier. I am adding an important condition to your standard probation orders. No part of your probation order shall override the best interest of this child. In the event you find the probation order conflicts with this child's best interest, you will obey my provision and notify the probation officer and ask for a hearing, if necessary. Further, you will try to enroll this child in Project Head Start for further language development.

"I would like to visit with you and the child on the first business day of the next two months for a few minutes at your residence after work if it does not conflict with your schedule. I request that Detective Lambchild accompany me with your consent.

"Adjourned."

David David reported back to the squad room. His new boss, Detective Ed Johns, was speaking with two detectives from another precinct. The two visitors enjoyed horrible reputations and were explaining that there was a need to do the sweep for bugs earlier than usual since there were reports of eavesdropping activity recently. No kidding.

The chief stepped out of his office and worked in the squad room while the two unsavory detectives closed the chief's door from the inside and swept the office for surveillance, more precisely while they retrieved the mayor's equipment now that his ploy to fire the chief had failed.

The chief watched the two depart without a word between himself and Ed Johns. It was clear that no squad room surveillance would be needed to find the mayor's myrmidons.

The chief returned to his office while Ed Johns spoke to the new employee. "There will come a time… Meanwhile, I want to assign you to their precinct for this next week. There is a murder case there, and the homicide detectives are new and need some help, mostly footwork. Also, keep your eyes and ears open but no bugs, understand?

"Meanwhile, what is your background?"

The chief's door was open, and his office and the squad room were very quiet.

"As a newborn, I was left on the park bench in front of the Mount Shiloh Baptist Church on the south side just before Sunday morning service. I was sort of adopted by the members and lived in all their houses. I was always called 'Lambchild' except one boy my age called me 'Christchild' because he was a little jealous. His father heard about that, and a spanking was scheduled.

"The boy told his father I had called him the N-word. The father said he did not think it wise to spank a white child but that his boy was fortunate because he was going to get a spanking. Then the boy told him that he might as well do it right since he had lied, that I had never used the word. The father told him that he was proud to have him as a son. The father said his son could trade his spanking for shaking my hand.

"I was always as well clothed and well-fed as any other child. I had dozens of parents and a host of brothers and sisters. All the unmarried ladies were my aunts. (He pronounced this word like people from Boston and Black people do, not like the insects at a picnic.)

"When I was five, a man from outside the neighborhood drove to a house down the street from me and began to demand favors of the young lady who lived there. She was not one of the ladies from the church, but I tried to help her. The man broke my arm, and when I fell down, he kicked me in the eye and took the girl with him. I went to the house of a basketball player and knocked on the steel-framed screen door. He took me to the hospital, where the doctors set my arm, put it in a cast, and x-rayed my eye. The bones were broken around my eye, which was swollen shut, but my eye was ok. They asked him many questions about who I was and whether he was the one who hurt me.

"When we left the hospital, he went first to a friend named Tommy who had just started his hair salon. I was on painkillers and slept on a couch at the hair salon while the basketball player got his very long hair cut in the middle of Saturday night or early Sunday morning. Then we went back to his house, where I slept on a couch. The following day he made me breakfast and took me to the house of Ms. Reba Washington, where I had been staying so I could dress for church. They had to cut my shirtsleeve because of my cast. Darius, the basketball player, told my Aunt Reba he would be back in one hour to take us to church. She did not believe him, but he did exactly that, dressed in a suit and tie. The church was packed. Everyone heard first that I was missing, then found but injured, and then saved by the tall young man.

"He put Ms. Washington and me in the front pew but sat in the very back. The people of Mount Shiloh are very kind and accepting and asked if he would like to speak. He stood and went to the very front. Instead of talking, he sang 'Amazing Grace' really well. Everyone joined. When they finished, he pointed at me and said, 'I drove, but he brought me here.'

"I might have lived in the neighborhood indefinitely, but something happened after the service. Everyone was on the front steps of the church when a car drove by very slowly. With my one good eye and my one good hand, I recognized the driver, my assailant, and pointed at him. He extended his arm across the front seat and pointed his hand formed like a pistol at me through his passenger window. He jerked his hand as if it had recoiled from a shot.

"The members had a meeting right then and decided it was time for me to be adopted partly for my safety. Darius, the basketball player, participated and agreed, saying it was almost time to register me in school and no one could legally register me.

"The neighborhood children got to speak as well and also agreed. I was treated just like every other child, same clothes, same food. One child said it was a shame since I could sing like a… When he hesitated, everyone took a deep breath until he said, 'like an angel of the curly persuasion.'

"One of the ladies knew Mrs. Lee and knew the Lees had lost their teenage daughter the year before. She said God would tell her what to say. We had to go to court for the adoption. They are now my parents but insist on being called my grandparents. They kept my last name to honor my giant, first family. 'Lambchild' is still the only name the people in the neighborhood call me. There was a placement party, and maybe my first family thought they would not see me again. The next Sunday and most Sundays since then, the Lees and I attend Mount Shiloh Sunday service."

Detective Johns said, "One piece of housekeeping—you will be called David. One week it will be in honor of your grandfather, and the next week it will be for your great grandfather. We will work on your cold case when you return."

David, formerly known as David David, handed him his file. "Oh, it's finished except for interviewing the alleged decedent. It can wait."

The cold case detectives were somewhat let down. In their comic camaraderie, they had already started calling each other John John and Sue Sue and telling each other, "The chief chief wants to see you."

David Lambchild was on his way to the precinct of two fairly new homicide detectives. It was also the precinct of the two odious detectives. The unmarked car David was driving had a spotlight on the driver's side like the one on the car of the man who had kicked him in the face. He knew who he was— the meaner and larger of the mayor's henchmen.

After introducing himself to the homicide detectives of his temporary precinct and learning from them what they wanted him to do, he worked with them until nearly six p.m. He was planning on making up his two court hours before going home.

At one point, he stopped for a restroom break. The meaner of the two slimy detectives rushed after him into the men's room. He shoved David against a black and white tile wall and kept him pinned there. With sheer hatred, he got right in David's face and said, "If you think your arm and your eye hurt last time, mention my name and I will put you in the ground."

David was not afraid of Detective Eliot, but he knew he would have to be dealt with. Permanently. No vicious person should be allowed to walk around with a weapon or the power that comes from being a detective. For that matter, he should not be walking around at all. If it had not been for his corruption and his badge, he would be doing time. David was not violent, but he thought about those words, "…In the ground."

Before the shift was over, those words were not only a threat but his solution–in the ground.

Hacking the internal affairs files on Detective Eliot and his partner, Detective Bain, would have been easy, but what would be the point of that? Besides, hacking the files would be illegal. He preferred his intricate plan. His father's humorous old saying came to him. "We never violate our standards, although we may lower them from time to time."

No, David's way would be a work of art. Complex, dangerous, exhausting, but conclusive. His initial estimate was that it would take one month, maybe five weeks, depending on how many crazy, talented friends he had. Later that timetable was drastically reduced by circumstances.

Every good plan has parameters. Eliot was guilty of years of violence, extortion, theft, and intimidation. Bain was not but backed Eliot. David actually wanted them to retire voluntarily. Killing them might be simpler and faster, but it would be personally burdensome, and it would put him on their level. Besides, their monthly retirement checks would allow but not guarantee their retirement from stealing as well.

He was assigned to this precinct for two weeks unless the current murder case was solved before that. He was sent to gather facts, check on alibis, interview witnesses or possible witnesses, meet family members of the murdered wife and of the suspected husband. The officers giving these assignments to him were green, no smarter or dumber than he was, and the assignments mostly made sense, so he was pleasant about going where he was sent and doing what he was told.

He was also doing daily surveillance on his two criminal detectives but never wrote or recorded anything. He knew where Detective Bain went on Wednesday afternoon and knew that Bain would die before divulging it. It was his only redeeming point but noteworthy.

For his assigned murder case, he had boxes of recordings and notebooks and pictures and diagrams, and by Thursday, he had too much to carry. It seemed he would never be given an office or even a desk wherever he went. He saw an interrogation room where one person was sitting at the far end of a table and decided to set his material at the opposite end of the table and work from there.

At a glance, David saw that the man at the table was in his forties, slightly overweight, unshaven with bloodshot eyes wearing a sweat-soaked light grey shirt and crumpled grey business suit. The man looked miserable and spoke almost as soon as David dived into his material. "I suppose they sent you in here to get my confession. I told them I would not give them one."

"I did not come in here to get a confession. In fact, I do not know who you are. No one is willing to give me a workplace, so I thought I could work here. I will leave if you like."

"No. Let me tell you what happened."

And so, he did. He told of how his wife and business partner were having an affair. That broke his heart, but he just really wanted to leave. His wife staged a scene at their pool when he got home from work. His partner, or rather now her partner, was hiding in the pump room that held all the supplies for the pool. Apparently, their plan was for her to provoke him into a rage, and when he became violent, it would be grounds for her to get more than half their community property in the divorce she anticipated. Her boyfriend would be on hand as a witness to the violence.

That did not happen. Instead, the boyfriend got bored while waiting in the small pump room and wanted to see if the pina colada tiki lamp fuel, which is really scented kerosene, really smelled like pina colada. It does, but when he squeezed the plastic bottle, the fluid poured down into the open box of chlorine powder and began making clouds of chlorine gas. The small room was already dark and was soon filled with gas. The business partner became disoriented and inhaled some of the gas fumes.

"We broke off our argument when we heard the crashing around in the pump room. EMS tried to help him, but his lungs were burnt. He still might survive.

"The elevator business is my separate property from before the marriage. The detectives claim they see a lot of motive for hurting my business partner, but nobody could have dreamed that up. I told them my wife could keep the house. I have been here since last night. I am really tired. If I am not under arrest, I am going home to pack."

"Goodbye. I'll tell them you left."

David was still organizing his own case when detested Detective Eliot and his accomplice entered the interrogation room.

"Where is my suspect?" The larger detective screamed so loud that everyone in the precinct squad room jumped up and came running.

"He said that since he was not under arrest, he was going home to pack."

Detective Eliot cursed at the top of his lungs. David suspected Eliot knew the man who left was innocent but saw a chance to shake down a man who owned a large elevator business.

Eliot was out of control. He was running around the end of the long table and about to attack the young detective in front of a room of witnesses. David David Lambchild drew his service revolver and pointed it at the center mass of the charging, enraged detective.

Eliot came to a halt feet from David and the barrel of David's weapon. David could actually see the broken veins in the older detective's nose caused by twenty years of heavy drinking. "You will not use God's name in vain again in my presence. Also, you will not attack me."

Retreating slightly from the pistol, he made a pistol of his own with his index finger and thumb. "We'll finish this later." He left without dignity but at least without bullet holes.

Not very bright in front of a room of police officer witnesses. The precinct captain saw and heard everything from the observation room on the other side of the see-through mirror. He had been there when the man explained the near-death of his partner. Both the statement by the elevator company owner and the outburst by the detective had been automatically recorded.

The case David was assigned to help with was fairly straightforward. The evidence he had collected enabled the two regular detectives to obtain a confession from the suspected husband the following day, Friday. The recent insurance policy, the acrimonious fights witnessed by family and neighbors, and the immediate travel plans for the husband and new friend uncovered by the regular detectives brought the case to a conclusion in time for David to return to the cold case squad the following week.

The squad was a little surprised to see him back so soon. Sue Jackson, formerly temporarily known as Sue Sue Jackson, spoke for the squad when she asked, "So how did you know that Harriet Meyer was not dead? She went missing ten years ago."

"I would like you to know how brilliant I am, but that will have to come later. She sent a postcard to a friend eight years ago. Somehow it found its way into her friend's player piano, which had not worked in years. One of my neighbors bought the piano recently, began restoring it, and found the postcard. It said she and her husband were going separate ways, and she was returning to her hometown. My neighbor showed me the postcard, and I located her."

David was mostly present, but part of him was asking how to put a person in the ground without putting him in the ground and how to build an elevator that doesn't move but seems to.

The chief had seen the video of the confrontation and wanted Detective Lambchild out of the office for a while, working on cold cases but in the field. He did not want any of his cold case squad embroiled in a feud with the mayor's favorites. Any person has the right to threaten deadly force to prevent bodily injury, and Lambchild showed professional restraint. On the whole, it would have been more convenient for the chief if Lambchild had just shot him, but the chief's true discipline showed through. He backed Lambchild, although he did not yet know the reason for Eliot's murderous hatred.

The mayor called and demanded that he fire the new detective. "I sent this guy to you for you to fire him, and you couldn't do it, could you? Now he has come close to killing one of our finest detectives."

The chief remembered the odious detective and the recent incident a little more accurately. "I am forwarding a video to you sent by the precinct captain. Please watch it and call me back. I believe this problem will be resolved very soon." *"Although I can't begin to guess how."*

"It had better be, or I will act, and you won't like it."

Soon after that conversation, the chief called in David David and his squad leader, Ed Johns. He had more confidence in Ed Johns than the mayor had in Detective Eliot but with far greater reason. Ed Johns was smart, honorable, and very resourceful.

"The mayor has just given me a very short amount of time to resolve the Eliot problem. Can this be resolved quickly?"

Ed Johns had seen the video. He did not want the death of this newest detective on his hands. He turned slightly to David David.

"With the help of the entire squad, I can guarantee one more cold case solved, and the Eliot issue resolved satisfactorily within seventy-two hours."

"No blood. Not yours, not his."

He nodded to the chief, then to Ed Johns. No one spoke, so they got up and left the chief to his thoughts.

———•———

The evening meal at the Lee's was very quiet, an unusual thing in itself. So unusual, in fact, that Mrs. Lee suggested that her husband and David David sit in the living room and talk while she cleaned up the dishes.

Mr. Lee had been a carpenter and furniture restorer but was mostly retired now. The loss of their daughter had almost destroyed each of them and their marriage. When the Mount Shiloh delegation first proposed the adoption in this very room, it seemed like such a good idea that Mr. Lee almost threw them out of the house. He was so used to his maudlin, paralyzing depression he had no way to console Mrs. Lee. Toward the end of that first visit, he watched in amazement as Mrs. Lee lifted her chin in defiance of all pain and depression and said, "I will agree if Mr. Lee agrees." She always called him Mr. Lee except when speaking to him. The room was super quiet. No one looked at Mr. Lee, afraid of his answer, until he said, "I agree." And that was before meeting the child.

Mr. Lee was thinking about that and about meeting that tiny boy with a swollen face and cast on his arm and about how David David lived with them during the six-month placement in preparation for the adoption. He remembered Mrs. Lee standing up to the judge and everyone else about the chosen name. They never stood a chance.

"What's bothering you?"

"I have to straighten out a wrong from the past concerning a dangerous person. It will require a lot of fast planning, almost magic, to trap him."

Mr. Lee thought for a long time. He thought of how David David had been their salvation and a tribute to their daughter. He thought how odd it was that they were chosen. Finally, he looked at David David, who was starting to worry about his silence, and thought about the problem.

"I don't know that I can be much help, son." He thought, "*What a great word — son.*" "I have always told you to do what you do best and go to the professionals and let them do what they do best. It sounds like you need a magician and a con man."

"Of course. The Pigeons. Thanks, Pop. You're brilliant."

"Glad I could help, son." Two of Mr. Lee's rules were to take the blame and apologize even when you don't know what you are accused of and the corollary, take the credit.

From the minute the door of the Pigeon household opened, David felt he was stepping onto a stage. He was greeted at the door that Monday night by three-year-old Samuel Pigeon with his mock glare. "Hey, David David." The child led him to the family room without another word as if he had been expected. He gestured silently and gravely to a chair like an impresario orchestrating the opening of an enormous Broadway show. Samuel nodded and exited, leaving David with the impression that the child had important production matters to attend to backstage.

The grandfather entered without making a sound. He took the chair across from David. He had never heard that any of the Pigeons worked, but the grandfather's suit looked conservative and very expensive. David suspected he had just dressed after Samuel notified him who was here. The gentleman exuded an aura of confidence. He had not spoken yet David felt as if suddenly he had been put under his spell. David's mind tried to formulate the words confidence man but rejected them as unworthy of his host.

He explained to Mr. Pigeon that he needed the impossible. He needed a very angry, dangerous man to think he had been transported several stories underground in an elevator, and then he needed that man to contact the police to rescue him. If possible, he wanted the man to be very near the mayor's office when he was "rescued" with his less evil partner nearby. The final requirement was that nothing done could be illegal. Mr. Pigeon stoically withheld a look of hurt and mentally moved the artistic demands of this production up a notch.

Mr. Pigeon finally spoke but did not say the idea was the worst he had ever heard or that it would be impossible. "We have done something like what you describe before and will be honored to be of service. I will be most like a casting director. I will interview each participant and will decide who does each part. My son and I will be behind the scenes in this product because we are known locally.

"The script is critical and is within my son's area of expertise."

As if waiting in the wings for his cue, the son glided into the room dressed in a tasteful suit and tie and took the remaining chair. David got the creepy feeling that the room had been arranged for three people even though he arrived unannounced. The father nodded toward David, apparently inviting him to repeat his request. David did so and explained further that he could not be the one to lure the angry detective into the trap since it had to be based on credibility blinded by greed, not anger.

The father and son exchanged glances conveying that they were impressed with David's insight. The son said the script dictated how many operatives or actors would be needed. "Aside from the final scene, I foresee that we need three actors, one for Detective Bain and two for Eliot. The keys to the success of this production are simplicity and plausibility. The flawed character of this detective will do everything else."

Roughing out the script followed, and it was agreed the Pigeons would provide two players and that David was to provide one unknown authoritative gentleman to be a chauffeur. He would ask Darius, the former basketball player, to help him choose someone. They agreed on no dress rehearsal.

Father and son stood in unison, and without any clear signal, Samuel entered and made a flourishing gesture toward the front door. Somehow David David felt older when he left.

The following day, Sue spoke for the squad. "We have been instructed to solve the Detective Eliot issue. What can we do to help?" David had methodically planned each step since leaving the surreal session with the Pigeons and was mostly organized.

"Here is what we need. Bain needs to be tracked all day today, hopefully without noticing. He is to appear at the mayor's outer office along with all of us and the chief at 4:30. He will have a handler, but he will then be turned over to me alone. It is important that he get off the elevator with all of us.

"Eliot will have two handlers. His temporary chauffeur will deliver him to the mayor's building with certain information and certain instructions. You will not meet the chauffeur. Eliot's second handler will be the elevator operator. You must have no comments about the elevator's operations or that for the day, there is actually an elevator operator. The operator will barely acknowledge the chief, and the chief will say, 'Long time, no see.' That will imply that the operator is an established member of the inner circle but not friendly with the chief. No one will comment that Detective Eliot is asked to remain on the elevator when we all exit at the floor for the mayor's office.

"It is imperative that all of us and Bain vacate the mayor's waiting room as fast as we get there. I will take Bain from there, and everyone else will go into the mayor's actual office.

"The mayor will arrive from an important meeting at 5:00. Everyone should be home in time for dinner."

At 8:30 that morning, Detective Eliot received a message from the mayor's office asking him to be there by 4:30 and asking him to call back and confirm as this was a matter of some importance. Earlier, the mayor had been informed that all past issues between the chief and the detective and Detective Lambchild and Detective Eliot were being resolved. The mayor was being asked to use his good offices as a neutral arbiter. The chief had told the mayor he wanted to give the mayor details about the endgame plan for the cold case squad at 5:00.

Detective Bain was called not by the mayor's office and told to be present at 4:30. His message hinted that the mayor was deciding today to dissolve the cold case squad, retire the chief, and possibly replace him with Detective Eliot. On behalf of the probable new chief, his task was to fire Detective Lambchild, so it was very important to stay with him. His handler was the one who called him. After great thought, it was decided by the Pigeons that his handler would be a female, professional but female. Her job was to make sure he communicated with Detective Eliot and indicate to him that the mayor's chauffeur would transport him for his appointment. Bain's handler indicated she had said too much and asked that Bain not report her lapse.

Darius's uncle was a retired marine visiting from Washington. His civilian job was chauffeur on high-profile security assignments. His new black Tahoe was used, temporarily bearing the plates borrowed from the mayor's garaged Tahoe. At 4:00 on the mark, he arrived at Detective Eliot's precinct. He told Detective Eliot that he was to provide transportation and security for the detective and turn him over to another member of his unit at the mayor's building. He told the detective he was not at liberty to say what the meeting was about.

This was said to confirm that only a weak member of the mayor's team would reveal the mayor's plan. The arrogance of Detective Eliot confirmed that the false information fed to Bain by his handler was received and believed.

"You don't need to worry. I have sources that are pretty good. I am aware of the agenda. I just don't know where the celebration will take place." The chauffeur acted as if only his duty prevented him from supplying this information.

The Pigeons had carefully selected Eliot's second handler. At lunchtime, the elevator was receiving routine maintenance. In fact, it was being equipped with sophisticated sound effects which would imitate the sound and vibration of a moving elevator. It had received a new elongated keypad. The bottom half of the floor numbers were behind a locked metal plate.

At 4:15, Darius's uncle handed Detective Eliot over to the second handler, who escorted him to the elevator. He explained that the mayor was nervous about his safety and wanted to meet with Detective Eliot in his identical office beneath the building, which was unknown to the public. Because he felt danger from the investigators and the chief, he misled them and had them meet in his upstairs office. The handler explained that the mayor would announce Detective Eliot's promotion to chief in his protected office, and so it would be over before anyone could do anything about it.

At 4:20, the investigators, Detective Bain, and the chief joined the two in the elevator. Everyone rode to the third floor. The chief said, "Long time no see" to the operator whom he had never seen before. Bain tried to stay on the elevator, but the surge of investigators swept him along with them to the mayor's outer office.

The elevator operator locked the elevator door and unlocked the lower portion of the keypad, which revealed negative numbers. The handler kept up a steady stream of information while the elevator supposedly descended to the third floor below the street. The operator explained that Eliot was to wait in the outer office of the mayor, who was to arrive in under five minutes.

In reality, the elevator had remained on the third floor despite the most convincing "ride." The chief and his investigators had gone into the mayor's office, locked the door, and remained silent. Bain had been escorted by David David Lambchild to an office down the same hall where he was giving Bain his true options.

"Within minutes, your partner will be fired by the mayor and arrested. I know you had no part twenty years ago when Eliot kidnapped and damaged a young woman the night he broke my arm. I know how every Wednesday, you care for the woman who was kidnapped and damaged. Because of that, you are being allowed to resign and retire. I will not reveal what I have just said to anyone ever, but you must resign. We have to wait for a few minutes and listen to the news."

A note on the desk of the outer office of the mayor was addressed to Detective Eliot. He saw it and read it. "You were going to put me in the ground?" Detective David David Lambchild signed it. Detective Eliot understood he had been tricked but thought he was trapped in the mayor's secret office under the building. He thought his best choice was to broadcast his situation on his police radio which was always monitored by radio and television stations.

Before the mayor had even arrived for what was supposed to be a peace treaty, television stations were broadcasting recordings of Detective Eliot's strange allegations and pleas for help. At his office's outer door, the mayor met a reporter from one station who asked for his comments about his detective's outcry. At the same time, he was handed Detective Bain's resignation.

When the mayor opened the outer office door, Detective Eliot tried to tell him they were safe in this underground office until the mayor's office door opened and the chief and his investigators poured out.

As his understanding grew, so did the detective's rage. The mayor could see in person the true character of his favorite detective, who was threatening to kill young Detective Lambchild of all people until Eliot's gun was taken at the mayor's request. The detective was then arrested for kidnapping a young woman missing since the night of David David Lambchild's injuries.

Naturally, the modifications to the elevator had vanished, the mayor's license plates were back on his Tahoe, Darius's uncle was on his way back to D.C., and the Pigeons' actor and actress had disappeared.

The mayor told the chief. "I do not want to hear any talk about dissolving the cold case squad. I have really had enough for a while. Lambchild, take him away," indicating the out-of-control Eliot.

Back in the normal-looking elevator again, David spoke quietly to former Detective Eliot. "I chose not to 'Put you in the ground' like you threatened to do to me, but for damaging a little boy and for kidnapping and damaging a young lady, at least I was able to put you three stories underground."

# MUD AND BLOOD

The teenage soldiers had been ordered to take no Western hostages. They had done exactly the opposite in their predawn raid of the farmhouse being used as a school and knew they might pay with their lives if they returned to the camp with the boy and the girl. The capture of the Westerners would bring soldiers to rescue them. A dozen children who were native would be used to show their parents that they were in the wrong religious group and needed to learn a lesson by paying money for their children's return. But the Westerners were to be left alone.

By the time the truck got to the refugee camp, the soldiers had thought they had come close to obeying their orders or at least correcting their first mistake. They had taken the two Western teenagers against orders, but then they thought they had killed them. The boy had been thrown out the back of the first truck, and his legs had been run over by the right double rear wheels of the second transport truck. He had disappeared under nearly a foot and a half of water and very soft mud. The girl had been struck in the face with a young guard's rifle butt so hard she had been knocked over the tailgate of the second truck and into the deep mud near the boy. She was stunned and still, which made her appear dead and prevented her from needing to be shot as the rocking trucks slowly disappeared down the muddy road in the heavy, unceasing rain. Later, the soldiers would have doubts about their solution and would come back to be sure the two were dead.

Her right cheekbone bore the brunt of the vicious blow. Fortunately, she was in near shock. Otherwise, searing pain would have prevented her from her task. With her partially open left eye, she searched for the body of the boy. The weight of the truck had pushed the boy's legs so far into the water and soft mud that the rest of his body was sunk too, and even his head was submerged.

His oversized lime green T-shirt was covered by the thick dark brown mud mostly. Part of the material floated on top of the water. She managed to crawl a few feet through the water and resistant mud to his head and lift it out of the water. Kneeling in nearly waist-high mud and water, she tilted his head back and pinched his nose. She bent over him and breathed into him three times while she was memorizing every feature of his face with her one good eye. He then began to cough and spray out the mud and water he had taken in all over her face, but the additional mud was not significant to her.

She was much smaller than he was but was wiry and indomitable. She dragged him off the road, which after three days of pouring jungle rain resembled a long trough. She thought his legs might be broken, so she pulled him by his arms and put him under a tree out of sight of anyone using the road. All evidence of them on the road was rapidly washing away in the steady rain. She was temporarily done in. She sat beside him, leaned against him, closed her eye, and slept.

When he got his bearings, he began to realize that he was propped against the green trunk of a tree, the name of which he did not know, and was sitting next to a fairly small girl with a smashed face. He vaguely realized she had revived him. His arrogant upbringing made him consider her action as unsolicited vulgarity. She had put her lips on his without his permission. Impertinence. He used the rain dripping down the huge thick leaves to wash his face a little. She was leaning against him as he took stock of her face. He recognized her as being from the embassy but did not know her or where she got the oval grid covering her right cheekbone. The very young soldier who imposed this grid would recognize the design of the metal plate on the butt of his rifle. The swelling of her cheek itself was minimal, although her right eye was swollen shut, and her bloody nose was evident. He could taste some of her blood from her revival efforts. He thought she looked like a pirate with the hashtag patch and shut eye.

He knew a person with a concussion should not sleep. He shook her and looked into her left eye when she awoke briefly. It looked clear, so he let her drift off back to sleep against him. Only then did he begin to check his legs by rotating his ankles very slightly. He would have tire marks across the front of both thighs for months where the blood had already accumulated under the skin if he lived that long. The mud had been very giving, and there was no serious damage.

As soon as both were awake and conscious, they started arguing.

Considering that she had just saved his life, his attitude was really cavalier. "It might be too much to ask, but, whatever your native language is, could we speak English?"

She responded sarcastically to his condescension, "Oh, do let's."

"I don't believe I care for your attitude, young woman. Do you know who I am?"

"No, and what's more, I don't care who you are. I am concerned with what you are, with what you are made of. Do you have it within yourself to help us get away from here before the soldiers start looking for our bodies? You know they will have to. Can you stand? The farm where we were captured is about five miles from here. I hid the embassy's satellite phone under the wooden steps of the front veranda just before being captured."

"If you are a servant, you are the most insolent one I have ever dealt with. And, yes, I can stand and walk, thank you. I would recommend that you wash up as I did, so we are no more conspicuous than necessary."

"If we are recaptured, we will only be conspicuous by our permanent absence."

She had enough of his arrogant remarks in a hurry. Within the first mile, she made three suggestions. "Grow up." "Stop being such a baby." "Put a sock in it."

He was in a little pain. His knees really hurt. Although his legs were operational, he was not thinking about those things. No one had ever spoken to him that way, pushing him, demanding of him the very most he was capable of, insisting they cover the entire five muddy miles by nightfall with no food.

The march was an all day, sloshing grind made slightly worse by the tension between them. They used the less muddy high edge of the road while it rained heavily, aware that they might have to hide quickly. They knew they would hear the low rumble of the soldiers' transport truck in time to dive into thick vegetation. The downpour erased their tracks as soon as they made them. They took two major breaks.

At about noontime, they moved off the road, and the boy started telling how normally he would be served his lunch by servants. Possibly he was implying who the servant was here. The girl could feel her pulse around her eye socket and by now was not even bothered by his remarks as long as he kept moving. They were both stiff from the rest, but within twenty minutes after the imaginary lunch break, they were each a little surprised at their progress and their stamina. At what would have been suppertime, they stopped again. They knew they were most of the way to the farm. The girl suggested that they remain standing so that they would not cramp up. Surprisingly, he did so without argument.

She knew they were within half an hour of the farm and knew they were almost completely spent. She handed him a chocolate candy bar. It was a little melted, and the wrapper was muddy and partially worn away. Totally unlike anything he had ever done in his life, he held it for a minute to see if she had a second one for herself. She did not, and he split it in half.

They were rescued from the farm she mentioned hours before the evil soldiers tracked them there. Marine guards from the embassy where she lived responded to her call. She told the marine sergeant, "I guess we should bring him along, too. He says he's important."

The boy seethed but thought she might find a way to leave him behind, so he "put a sock in it."

• • •

Astrid was on the upper cobblestoned veranda of a private home offered for the use of the American ambassador in Athens. It overlooked the second level, crowded with dinner tables which in turn overlooked a beautifully manicured lawn and garden below. A sumptuous seafood dinner for a large number of diplomats and their families had finished, but some lingered. Although her father discouraged it, she was helping the staff clear the last tables. They had worked hard all day to prepare the grounds, the tables, and the Mediterranean meal and now wanted people to go home, so they could eventually get to bed.

She heard two young men talking near a dinner table on the second level of the veranda. The first had said, "Blood <u>is</u> thicker than water." The younger man said, "So is mud." The world stopped. Without thought of what appeared to be her humble status as a waitress or his apparent wealth, she descended the steps to the second level of the veranda, approached him, stood right in front of him, between him and his friend. She looked directly at his face and studied it.

"Mud?"

"Blood, is that you?"

The original speaker had lost any hope of understanding why the son of such a prominent family would allow one of the servants to initiate a conversation on such familiar and peculiar terms. He decided on a final drink instead of solving their social puzzle and, without another word, headed for the weary bartender's station.

"Well, of course, it's you. Who else has a faint hashtag on her cheek?"

She said nothing else but continued to study every feature of his face. It was clear she was in love. Finally, looking at his tuxedo, she said, "I see you've changed your shirt. The other was probably too stained to salvage."

The American ambassador approached the table to suggest that Astrid finally stop working. This was the ambassador the boy had bragged of knowing so well on their long, muddy march together.

The young man said, "Mr. Ambassador, you may recall me. I am Shedrick Quinton."

"Yes, and I see you've met my daughter, Astrid."

Astrid batted her eyes at Shedrick, conveying that her relationship with the ambassador was as much a surprise to her as it was to him. He barely avoided glaring at her for withholding this important piece of information. That explained why the marine guards from the embassy had arrived to save them so promptly. Until this moment, he thought she was the daughter of one of the lesser clerks at the embassy.

"Why don't you two go down into the garden and catch up while I close this party down?" The ambassador was aware of the ordeal they had shared and thought it wise to allow them a chance to get reacquainted. Shedrick was breathless as they descended the stone stairs to the garden level. He sounded as if he had been running even as they sat on a low stone wall and shared a companionable silence for a few minutes. Finally, with a slightly wicked smile, Astrid said, "If you are having trouble breathing, I could help you again."

He turned red and, with fake dignity, said, "Such impertinence from a servant girl." They both laughed. He told her that her eye had healed beautifully. She thanked him and told him, "You are different somehow."

"I know. My friends tell me that I seem to have grown up ten years in a month." Then he added, "Thank you."

———•———

They saw a great deal of each other following the embassy dinner and found that they really liked each other. Neither had future plans, and both needed work. Even the money they were spending on today's coffee and cake in a humble cafe was from their allowances. Shedrick had come a long way, but Astrid thought manual labor was still not in the picture. Shedrick thought that their strength was in their knowledge of the vast number of families within the State Department and in their understanding of the machinery of their part of the government.

Astrid added to this idea. "We know how to cut the red tape and could generally be like a two-person concierge for State Department employees and their families. We could be problem solvers."

It was several weeks before they were summoned. The ambassador had heard of their vague plan. He asked them to his office, gave them tea, and generally acted like he had all afternoon to visit. He did not. He was evaluating them for an assignment. He was deciding whether they could work as a team. He thought so, but he asked them anyway.

Shedrick spoke for them both after a quick look at Astrid. "Yes."

Astrid confirmed simply by crossing her fingers and saying, "Mud and blood."

"You still have time to back out. The son of one of the native clerks of the embassy is accused of killing another citizen in Ethiopia. I want you to find out as much as you can. You will have no authority and must stay on the good side of the local police. Unless you change your minds, you will leave tomorrow. Expect to be gone two weeks. You will stay at the embassy in Addis Ababa and work as civilian assistants to families of the State Department. You do not have to solve the murder, but you can gather background information that might be overlooked.

# THE GROUP

Two brindle squirrels are resting on the topmost branches of a pine tree on a high hill, the third along the eastern entrance to the Gila Wilderness. Their fur is being blown gently by the southwestern breeze while they enjoy a spectacular late spring view. They look down the dusty, red road that leads into the wilderness campground. They can see, across the road through the pine needle haze of tree branches, a panorama of scrub oak and juniper trees and occasional spindly ocotillo. The fragrant pines and piñon are sprinkled throughout open areas, mini meadows of tall yellow and green grass, highlighted by the afternoon sun. The squirrels have nowhere to go and nothing to do. They are caught up.

They hear the distant drone of an engine climbing the second hill, the one before theirs. The engine suddenly relaxes as the yellow bus crests the second hill and begins its descent. The driver shifts into low gear to climb the third, the steepest hill. The young passengers alternate between screaming collectively for no intelligent reason and darting to the left side of the bus, trying to catch their first glimpse of the Gila River.

The riverbed is much wider than the present river. Huge cottonwoods and gum trees have fallen as the river changes course from side to side — a restless, noisy sleeper in a king-sized river bed. The eager children catch abbreviated views of a dotted line of golden splinters—the Gila. They cannot yet see small, lightweight loaves of pastel river rocks— tan, brown, green, grey, red—worn smooth by thousands of years of rapidly charging water. The river is still too far away to be heard over the noise of the occupants of their vehicle.

The bus carries thirty-six emotionally charged, emotionally challenged children and their counselors, the hopes of two school districts, and the hopes of the few families of the children who are not orphans. The school districts' hopes range from pleasant and noble to unpleasant. Most hope the children and those who run the center will return to the city refreshed and happier and calmer. They would settle for law abiding. Some are just grateful for a few days of rest. A few hope the children never return and do not care about the details.

The children are a remarkable collection of orphans and emotionally disturbed from a center changing from an orphanage to a psych center five hours away from the Gila Wilderness. Several children are transitioning from the orphanage into the new program since they are emotionally disturbed orphans. For now, it is the only children's psych center from Denver to Mexico City, from Phoenix to Dallas.

All eight members of cottage two's notorious group are on the bus. Among them is one passenger whose own seat only occasionally makes contact with the bus seat, an eleven-year-old with braces and straight brown hair apparently controlled only by static electricity. He earned a place at the center and at the table of cottage two for an incident with a train that ran beside a park during a suddenly abbreviated picnic originally in his honor.

Another group member, only a year older, spent his first four years raised as a pet on the floor of a home in a foreign country and his last four years as the youngest child in a state mental hospital in the United States, often injected with Thorazine to control him. His sole rule for survival at the hospital is well remembered— "Always get even; everyone sleeps sometimes." Even teenagers with major mental disorders came to understand that. He escaped the mental hospital for a visit to the city and broke into the juvenile detention center, gaining the attention and fury of the juvenile court judge and earning a place at the table of cottage two in lieu of jail. He has rare episodes where he is devoid of any emotion. The head counselor tells the staff it takes about four hours of encouragement for him to overcome this flatlining of emotion. One counselor secretly delights in wrecking his day and pushing him to despair. The child plays the guitar and sings very well. He resents the label "superficially charming." He is damned charming.

John and Cody are seated directly behind the driver and are not technically enrolled in the center. They are the youngest the center has dared to accept and are coming into the center because their home alternatives would almost certainly be fatal. They are under the protection of the driver, Super Two, and more importantly, under the protection of cottage two, the group.

A consortium of hard-nosed businessmen and bankers, and doctors fund the center after one most inspiring meeting with the administrator of the sisters of the Incarnate Word. History tells of a private meeting between Attila the Hun and Pope Urban, after which Attila chooses not to sack defenseless Rome and returns to eastern Europe with his vast marauding army. The bishop, after a meeting with the Incarnate Word administrator, allows the consortium to create a psych center and use the orphanage facilities and its twenty acres closely surrounded by furrowed, irrigated cotton fields.

That same administrator is personally overseeing this outing and uses it for many purposes: fun, training counselors, letting the city rest for a few days. Roman roads and Egyptian pyramids were planned with the same attention to detail undertaken by the center on the road to accreditation as a psych hospital. The hiring of Super Two and the other cottage supervisors, and this camping trip, are part of that long-range plan.

The children overwhelmingly indicate they are "way" ready to get off the bus. Super Two, the driver, would have agreed back at the squirrels' tree— and they explode from the bus into an organized, structured campsite with the smell of spaghetti and garlic rolls all created by the advance team to welcome them. Consistency in the face of change. Very Important.

Dinner is served at the same time by the same people. Milieu therapy may have a more technical meaning, but at the center and wherever the center goes, it means that the therapists help cook and garden and that the cooks and gardeners are all part therapists for every child, and they travel with the center. Structure. Consistency. Milieu therapy and more structure.

The advance team has raised large tents for three of the four cottages. The tent for cottage two is neatly folded at its tent site, and its tent poles are still back at the center. The group, immediately convinced of sabotage, begins scanning the campsite for recipients of their retaliation. Super perceives the early clouds of war and, as the head counselor of cottage two, convenes a meeting of the group.

The group governs the cottage and progresses as a group or suffers the consequences as a group. Punishments and rewards within the cottage are usually decided by the group even when the decision differs from the staff's. When it fails to act responsibly, the group suffers the natural consequences as a group, as a government. It moves as a group, protects as a group, eats as a group, travels as a group—peer pressure for progress.

Only when justly protecting a member of the group are the group members allowed their favorite saying, "I have eight guys who can make you leave us alone." It is the only cottage where the group members are punished for not fighting when the cause is just, no matter how big the opponent, no matter how inevitable the outcome. This doesn't happen between cottages normally since each cottage has a chain of command, a pre-battle appeal process.

It is decided with minimal input from Super that the night will be cold and they need their tent and that tent poles are for mere mortals. The waxed canvas tent is unfolded and laid on its side on a bed of pine needles, and their gear and sleeping bags are slid into this long, tan canvas envelope. It will keep out the ground moisture and hold in their heat and safeguard them from possible rain. It is agreed their two small protected guests will sleep in the center of the tent, in the center of the group.

Everything is pre-planned when possible. "We are going camping. We will travel for five hours. We are taking two guests. They are members of the group during the campout. If you hurt them, you pay. If anyone else hurts them, you pay. Does anyone want to prevent the group from going camping? Volunteers? Last chance. Come on." Preemptive humor.

At each "cottage," every child's travel bag is beside his or her sleeping bag. There is one girls' cottage, or, in this case, tent, and three boys', the national ratio of institutionalized children. For imprisoned adults, too.

The fragrance of pine and piñon trees mixes with spaghetti and garlic bread. There is also salad and bug juice, apparently a camp name requirement for referring to the red punch. Just before the meal, the counselors convene their own public meeting, and a phony, heart-wrenching request is made to the children for a volunteer to wreck the meal with a tantrum or some "acting out." The staff apologizes for such short notice. Humor and spirit are good countermoves against most mind games, especially when used preemptively. Always a dangerous ploy, but the counselors are taught that a child will test limits adroitly when doing so unconsciously and that the best way to extinguish a particular habit is to ignore it and to encourage the child to consider acting out the same behavior consciously.

The children nod to one another or make eye contact, smiling tolerantly. They have heard this corny routine before and still think it is funny. They are included in something that involves getting attention but no punishment. It's about belonging and sharing. Running gags are constant. "The zoo called. The gorilla is ill and needs a substitute. Anybody?" Lighthearted jokes about the staff are fair game. Almost the entire staff are called by their first names only: no Mister, no Miss. The nuns are "Sister..." followed by their first name.

Announcements throughout the next few days continue, saying that if no one volunteers to mess up, someone will be appointed, or worse, a counselor will have to act out. The counselors are nurturing and encouraging, mostly. And so corny. Corny is not threatening.

Each new child eats like he or she is never going to see another meal. Once a child knows where the next meal is coming from and that it will even be on time, his or her appetite slowly gets closer to that of a normal child. Not Cody, the smaller of the two protected guests of the group. He always eats like a small bird and drinks water like he is headed for a year-long trip across all the deserts of the earth—so much water.

The sun appears to be resting briefly on a distant hill shining through the lower branches of an ancient gum tree west of camp. The nuns and cottage counselors have put large name tags on each child's sleeping bag. Territory (personal space) and possessions are very important to the insecure, and clear ownership prevents fights.

A few children, secure in their possessions, use their time to make remarks about where the male and female counselors will sleep. The single directive, "Inappropriate," is often used without punishment or further comment. Children with brain damage or emotional problems respond best to short, clear, encouraging imperatives, not sermons and not anger. Besides, the children know that the administrator deals with inappropriate behavior among the well-trained, meagerly paid staff even faster than the staff deals with the children. There will be no staff hoochy goochy, as the smaller children call it.

The dry mountain air retains none of the day's heat and cools rapidly. The children dive into their well-marked gear for their sweaters and jackets. Each cottage, including staff, takes turns helping prepare the meals and cleaning up afterward. Everyone helps clean up the first night and knows there will be a campfire afterward. The staff stretched it by commenting that the children had the opportunity for a meltdown but missed it.

The next few days will be as tightly organized as days at the center from breakfast until bedtime, just like always. Hiking, archery, rafting, and woodcraft are all supervised, five to one, kids to counselors. Even at the campfire, the counselors are constantly counting their assigned kids, especially at the campfire. Every counselor is taught that fire starting is one of the three red flags indicating deep disturbance along with bedwetting and torturing small animals. Four, if you count biting humans. Yes, four.

The campfire is a magical time. Some of the children are amazing storytellers and weave some truth into the stories, most encouraged by the staff, stories of thoughtful, very smart children who overcome all obstacles. One child says that he used to be thirty-two with two bright children but that he is getting younger and younger and that pretty soon he will not even be born yet. The staff started to panic, but one of the other children simply asked where he got such a strange idea. The storyteller said that Merlyn the Magician who raised King Arthur and lived backward in time had been on a rerun of Lost in Space recently.

The staff stories are always about functional families with caring parents and brilliant children. The American termite family always seems to find itself homeless but always finds a new home and a new beginning thanks to the father's wisdom. The name of that story is "Father Gnaws Best." If any part of this story is left out, the children insist it is told. One child who originally felt like an outsider kept adding to the story. "Are you saying the children actually ate the family out of house and home?" "Did their relatives really come out of the woodwork?" "Was it really dangerous for the children to say, 'I'm bored/board?'" This storytelling gives the older children the chance to teach the younger children who are sometimes ashamed of learning itself.

As the fire dies down, the children ask, "Do we still get a nighttime snack?" The administrator is convinced that if the entire staff was wiped out in a cataclysm, the children's question would remain the same. First, the staff had to go through a big routine about who was supposed to bring the snacks and was that counselor bright enough for the assignment. But, of course, even at camp, there is a nighttime snack, and much encouragement as the children begin to retire. Food is a big part of nurturing. Even the newest counselor knows that a child who goes to bed relatively happy hopefully gets eight hours of therapy and a head start on the next day.

One child arrived at the center straight from a children's hospital. His doctor forbids him to return home for as much as a blanket before coming to the center. His bleeding ulcers and manipulative behavior endanger his life and almost kill his parents.

At the hospital:

Calling home. "If you love me, you'll call me right back."

Calling the hospital. "Oh, baby, we love you."

"Who is this?"

"Your mother. You said to call if we love you."

"I never called you. Stop calling." Disconnect.

Calling home. "If you love me, you'll call me right back." Click.

Calling the hospital. "Oh, baby, we love you."

"Who is this?"

This and a dozen other games go on until the psychiatrist hears about it. He bans all communication with the family for ninety days. The boy attends services at a chapel of his religion near the center in the company of Super Two. If he is not showered and ready to go on time, Super tells him afterward how especially nice the congregation was and how delicious the food was at the light meal afterward.

A place at the table easily, but he brings to the table more: he is a beginning magician, a humorous and amazing storyteller, and a track star. He tells the other students at his public school that the reason he is at the center is that he is crazy, so naturally, everyone likes him.

The base of the actual much-discussed table of cottage two is a salvaged cable spool cut down to standard table height. Two thick pieces of plywood are bolted to the spool side by side and cut into an oval to accommodate all the group and staff. A furniture swivel supports a large circle of wood in the center that rotates since no one can reach all the way across the table. The members of the group could pass things to each other by spinning the wheel.

From that table, they are taught in short, imperative phrases to plan (to replace impulsive behavior). Their chant is part of the plan.

"What do we do?"

"Plan."

"When something comes up, and there is no plan, what do we do?"

"Plan now."

"When there is an emergency, what do we do?"

"Plan fast."

By the third day of the campout, the children are recovering from their temporary disorientation and are returning to various, old, reliable methods of acting out, of proving low self-esteem.

The counselors and the group are countering with private conferences, spontaneous group-decision meetings, and time-outs.

Ram is in cottage two and could compete in the world finals for the unlovable child. How he came to the center is its own story, to be told separately. For now, it is sufficient to say his doctor declared him brain dead after what Ram thought was a series of unfair questions meant to prove he was severely mentally challenged. The group agreed he was challenged and that the questions were unfair then voted to accept him. The staff backed the group and said he was a salvageable disaster. The doctor capitulated but kept a close eye on Ram. And Ram was constantly on guard for more unfair tests.

At this moment, Ram is facing a tree and is in time out for calling another camper's mother a pig. Group decision. A five-minute time out allows him time to calm down and reconsider his action. If he messes up during the time out, he starts his time over. Sometimes his time out is open-ended. After tripping another football player, he is told, "When you are ready to play fair, bring yourself back into the game." This works for all the children, and they know when they are ready. It is the most economical system. Most children only punish themselves as much as they need to. It allows them to change their own attitude and save face by not being seen as changing their attitude too quickly.

One of the group has lost both his parents to violence. For months he was incapable of grief, but he is amazing. He collects from his two younger sisters their allowance before Mother's Day for flowers for their mother's grave and the same for their father. He "borrows" the mother of one of the counselors to show respect for a mother on Mother's Day. That made the counselor cry. He acted out, kicking people in the leg, children and counselors both. Super told him, "One more time, and I will take you over my knee and spank you with my hand." Almost immediately, the child kicked him in the shin. The spanking was almost symbolic since it did not hurt, but when the child saw Super sitting there frustrated afterward, he came back and hugged Super and cried and said, "Thank you. Thank you. No one has spanked me since my mother died. She always told me, 'Don't be a donkey.' Thank you. Thank you."

The counselors consider investigating who told the children about the field of Indian pottery shards near the campsite. The field is down a trail to the river, past two huge fallen trees that have to be climbed over, across a deep arroyo and atop a large, loamy mesa a quarter mile from camp. The tiny tunnels dug by an army of animals that look like small marmots keep the topsoil soft.

There is enough time before the evening meal on the third day to make it there and back without making the group late for the meal, and John and Cody, the protected guests, know it. The older kids' day hike is planned to give enough time to return and rest before the meal of fried potatoes, ranch-style beans, and hamburgers. The two smallest campers are hounding Super Two to go with them and promising they will not be too tired to walk back to the campsite and promising they will not ask to be carried. The fascination of finding a broken piece of pottery with part of a pattern of the Jornada or the Mugillons (Mug—ee-owns) or the cliff dwellers is ecstasy to them.

It is a federal violation to remove shards from the Gila Wilderness. The two have been good while visiting their friends, the shards, about putting them back, but each is insisting in his own way on visitation rights.

It is almost too much for Super Two, just back from a five-mile all-day hike with the always charming adolescent campers, to picture carrying the two unhappy visitors (They must each weigh more than a backpack). They are sure they cannot survive without visiting their friends, the shards, before dinner and sunset.

"No, John. No, Cody. You guys will ask me to carry you all the way back." Together they are only fourteen years old, but they are formidable. They would not be at the camp at all, but the orphanage/psych center administrator had a second idea besides camping. Why not invite the two boys in shelter care for their pre-placement visit? The child/staff ratio would still be appropriate, and this four-day trip could serve as their orientation.

John and Cody respond in different ways to the damages of rejection, neglect, and abuse heaped upon them. Cody withdraws and drinks more water. Supposedly medically doomed, developmentally delayed, brain-damaged, and frail, but always quiet with small bursts of wisdom. John, on the other hand, always explodes with energy, denial, or anger. Even at his age, his reports carry the words" volatile" and "labile" (slipping from one mood to another easily). When really hurt, his stock expression is, "It doesn't hurt."

Both at this moment have backed against a fallen tree trunk facing the counselor, their only hope to the top of the mesa. Good camper, bad camper in miniature. Super Two is twenty-two with youth's inexhaustible ability to rebound and with a rapidly weakening ability to say no to the two before him. He approaches the huge log the two boys are leaning against and sits in the dirt before them to be at their eye level and crosses his legs like an Indian and locks on each face for a moment and then asks with mock seriousness, "John, Cody, do you guys have to go pottery?"

Cody's top-heavy, egg-shaped head tilts to the left and his right eyebrow arches up, and a small smile appears. John folds his arms on his small chest and pronounces, "I not laughing." Cody pats John on the shoulder like he would a Labrador and smiles again. Their shard visit goes very well.

Super Two slept just up the hill above the canvas envelope beneath New Mexico's twinkling blanket of stars and pondered how many stars there are and how many have names and drifts off and dreams of orphan stars with odd names and how their brilliance is arriving after the star is already gone. And as these two orphan stars begin their night's sleep therapy, Cody receives his task, for it is during this dream and during the end of this trip that Super Two formulates the idea to use Cody as a time capsule to help both Cody and John, christened forever in his heart, "the mini group."

Because of his "drinking problem" with water, Cody has to use the restroom built by the National Park Service a few years before and very conveniently located tonight. Super sleeps lightly and hears Cody getting restless and wraps him in his own jacket, and illuminates the path with his own flashlight. Cody says he can take care of business without help, and so he waits for Cody outside the restroom. Super is tired, but the alternative is unthinkable. Cody's sleeping bag is in the center of the sleepers in their canvas envelope as the group ordained. The eight members of the group will protect him from all outsiders, but none of them want to find out if bedwetting is one of Cody's problems. Tonight tragedy is avoided.

Just as Cody is back in his bag conking out, he smiles sleepily and says, "Good night, Tyler."

No other child or staff save one knows Super's name. His name has never been used for very good reason. Only the one who hired him, the administrator, knows his real name, and it has never been repeated. Super is temporarily speechless, and Cody is asleep before the response. "Good night, Cody."

Super Two, formerly known as Tyler, was one of the van drivers for a different center near Austin, which cared for profoundly mentally challenged children. Many of the children had underdeveloped lungs, and each summer were driven to the clean air of Guadalajara, Mexico, in three vans. They were present at the airport, picking up one of their doctors in late May when Juan Jesus Cardinal Posadas Ocampo was sitting in his large, black car in the parking area and was caught in the crossfire of a drug war and was killed. A cardinal of the Catholic Church, his large, black car may have been mistaken for that of one of the targets.

The barrage of bullets was horrible. The director of that facility said simply, "Tyler, we have to get these children out of here." Cody was in Tyler's van and heard and never forgot that simple directive. Tyler had transferred to the new center across the vast state for self-preservation and so as not to bring harm to these children, he never used his real name.

Cody had originally been placed at the center near Austin, but the placement was temporary since his speech and memory were so good. Too good in this case. He could repeat everything he heard and saw during the gunfight and often did, just like a parrot.

Throughout this camping trip, Cody recites long stories with childlike simplicity, stories he hears at church and stories he hears on the radio. As a result, the children and counselors call him "the Codester," "the Code Master," "the Code Meister." The "Code Meister" sticks.

John can never tolerate an entire story except one by Cody, and Cody can never resist or forget one and can recite it just as he heard it months or years later, even when the meaning of the story is beyond him. Super Two tells the Code Meister stories of encouragement and direction, knowing John will hear them later when he needs them.

Over the next five years, the group members outgrew the center and went home or into foster care or into programs for older children or were adopted. A family wanted to adopt one child, the one who collected allowance for flowers from his sisters for their deceased parents, but he said he could not leave since he had to watch out for his two sisters. That family adopted all three. One child grew and went into law enforcement later and was partially responsible for thwarting a train robbery of new denim jeans. The bandits had come across the border from Mexico at Anapra in New Mexico, and he heard one say in Spanish, "This will be easy. The fat one will never run fast enough to catch us."

When he put the cuffs on the speaker, he said, "I've got eight fat guys who say you will not rob this train."

This chapter in the group's life comes to an end, but clearly, their book is not finished, and most of them reappear at various stages of their lives. Some would never have another family but did form a bond to carry them through their lives.

# THE HOBBY SHOP

He knew the two were up to no good the second they entered his shop. Well-dressed and barely polite, it was obvious they were not interested in anything in the shop. He knew all about them. He knew who had sent them and what they wanted. He almost rolled his eyes.

Various shopkeepers were being shaken down by the neighborhood's newest crime boss: five percent of their net profits in exchange for the new boss's protection. It would also involve having someone monitor the books to see that the shopkeeper was being honest about being robbed.

He did not want to go back to the old ways, although they were very effective. He now had a wife and granddaughter to consider. But he had to act fast. Just damaging or eliminating the two who had been sent would be short-sighted. This was a monumental opportunity. He decided he had to deal with their boss. Old Rule One: Never send or receive messages. Go to the source. He had already done his homework.

The two were delivering their message. As if by mistake, they had begun knocking over displays of models and building materials needed for solar energy projects. The Stirling engine had been knocked to the floor.

"Some of your merchandise is not very stable. It seems to us you need all kinds of protection."

"Yeah, we're having a special on earthquake protection," the second hood indicated as he knocked small jars of butyrate paint for models onto the floor with his elbow. They were plastic and did not break.

The hobby shop owner got very close to them. They had never seen him before. Even though he was seventy, he was physically very impressive, barrel-chested with powerful arms. He spoke quietly, making direct eye contact and calling them each by name. Old Rule Two: Do your homework.

"Aldo. Benjamin. When you finish cleaning up your small accidents, you might want to look around to familiarize yourself with the inventory. You may wait on anyone who comes in. The cash register is unlocked. I have an errand across town on Monroe Street. When you leave, please close the door. You do not need to lock it. The neighborhood is very safe." By no coincidence, their boss lived on Monroe Street. He knew they knew and knew where he was headed.

He passed through a doorway at the back of his store where his family lived. There he spent about fifteen minutes. He assisted his wife, helping her prepare for the afternoon. It was lunchtime, but not for him. He was on a mission. He passed through the store wearing a large hat that covered his bald head. Without even looking at the two young thugs, he walked out the front door.

He got off the bus on Monroe Street on the block of his destination. He removed his large hat and rang the doorbell of a large two-story house, and waited. A woman in a maid's uniform opened the door but did not speak.

"I would like to speak to Mr. Angelo."

She looked at him but again did not speak. She left him standing at the front door. She left the door open and went away. Next came a very strong young man, bristling. He spoke. "How can I help you?" His tone contradicted his question.

"I am here to see Mr. Angelo."

The young man's job apparently was to frighten away anyone who came to the door. The shopkeeper was not frightened. He had made his appraisal and decided that this young man would not be a problem if the old ways prevailed.

"Mr. Angelo does not want to see you. You have received his business proposition. There is nothing to discuss."

"I do not deal with messengers or agents. I have a counterproposal for Mr. Angelo which I will only discuss with him."

The "muscle" might have thought he could impress his boss by scaring this persistent man away. He studied him, trying to decide how much effort it would take to rough him up in his short-sleeved white shirt and blue bow tie and then throw him in the gutter. He decided it would take quite a bit.

Forestalling the bodyguard's possible plan, the shopkeeper said, "I do not speak for Mr. Angelo, but I would not want a scene in front of my own house. If you do not succeed in throwing me off the property, it would be embarrassing for you and perhaps for him. When I was subject to someone else's authority, my rule was always to leave the boss his options. In this case, he may like my counterproposal."

The door remained open, and the bodyguard walked away, leaving the shopkeeper still standing at the front door.

After a few minutes, the large bodyguard returned and said, "Mr. Angelo will see you in the living room."

The shopkeeper simply followed the bodyguard into the first room in the house, which was richly furnished. Almost everything was some shade of light yellow and tasteful. He did not sit but stood holding his large hat.

A man in his forties came in wearing an expensive suit. "I am Mr. Angelo. You received my business proposition and yet have not accepted it. I do not make exceptions. Unless there is something else, we are finished." The large bodyguard began to move toward the shopkeeper.

Totally unintimidated, the shopkeeper ignored the bodyguard except to consider his physical strategy toward him, if necessary. He bowed to Mr. Angelo. "My name is Robert Costa. I, too, make no exceptions and do not give anyone money for no reason. I respect your policy and have a counterproposal which I think will suit both of us. Everyone involved is cordially invited to my family's house behind the hobby shop this evening. You and Mrs. Angelo are most humbly invited to a meal being prepared by my devoted wife whom I would like your wife to meet. This gentleman and the two young men I met at my shop today are also invited. I want the two young men and this gentleman present because my proposal involves them. I hope to see you at seven."

From a crime boss's point of view, this was a terrible idea. To allow an exception to his policy, getting familiar with the person being extorted, accepting an invitation, mingling with the family. On the other hand, his wife never gets a chance to meet anyone in town considered respectable and is growing more and more isolated. Also, the very odd part was that the shopkeeper was not in the least intimidated by his two young visitors, by his enforcer, and not by any of the horrible consequences that anyone knew would follow non-compliance with his "offer."

Promptly at seven, Mr. and Mrs. Angelo and the three employees arrived at the hobby shop. The lights were on, the sign on the door said open, so they all went inside. Mrs. Angelo's comment on how very tidy the shop was earned the two younger employees a freezing look from their boss.

Mr. Costa came through a door at the rear of the shop wearing the same white shirt and bow tie and now a sports coat. Everyone was invited to enter to meet his family. Mrs. Costa was introduced, as was their granddaughter, Julia, who was very shy. She appeared to be about ten and appeared to have Downs Syndrome. Mrs. Costa was in a wheelchair and was removing her apron.

Although the entrance was a little unusual, everything after that reflected the good taste of Mrs. Costa and the order of her husband.

"Mrs. Angelo, could you help me check on the salad, the bread, and the Chicken Jerusalem? Julia, could you invite the young men to serve everyone drinks? Don't be shy. They are very nice. Just do what we practiced. Serve Mrs. Angelo first, then the men, and no wine for anyone under twenty-one."

The living quarters took up all of the first floor of the building that the hobby shop did not occupy. The ladies left the living room, passed through the dining room where an antique oak table was set for dinner and entered a beautiful kitchen where the counters accommodated a person in a wheelchair. Not just the counters but the cabinets and the refrigerator, also. "My husband built me a spice garden here at the end of the kitchen." After checking on the bread and the Chicken Jerusalem, she wheeled into an alcove where rows of black lights bathed basil, rosemary, mint, and oregano.

Mrs. Costa did everything to make her guest feel completely at home. "Please call me Mari." While cutting mint for the tea and basil for the salad and handing them to Mrs. Angelo, who was putting them into bowls, Mrs. Costa told her, "My husband says he has done his homework in planning this evening. He wants to make your husband a business offer that is generous and legitimate. He has chosen Mr. Angelo for his skills. Beyond that, I know nothing about the business except that it is honorable. This is a great night.

"Personally, he makes me feel there is no one else on earth he would rather be with. Whatever he wants to do, I support him with my being. We are hoping to return to my native Tuscany."

In the other room, the shopkeeper and Mr. Angelo finished their glasses of wine, and Mr. Costa's guests were invited back into the hobby shop. "I mentioned a counterproposal which is only a small part of an idea I have. With Mr. Angelo's consent and only after a year of apprenticeship under Mr. Angelo's management, I want to offer twenty-four percent of the shop to each of your young assistants. Rather than protect the store, they will own a minority share of the store. Again, only with your consent, I want your larger assistant to own the remaining fifty-two percent after one year under your supervision.

"I understand that your background is in chemistry. The enforcer stared and waited for his boss to put this shopkeeper in fear of his life, although he was right about his extensive chemistry background.

Mr. Angelo did not want to ruin the dinner for the sake of his wife. For now, he would suavely deflect these little job offers to his employees and defer enforcement to a time when his wife was not present.

Mr. Angelo spoke with courtly, polished manners but was reserved. "Your offer to relieve me of my three employees, I respectfully decline. I chose them and need them to enlarge my business."

Acting like he was deaf, Mr. Costa said, "You have not heard my proposal yet. I would like to give you a tour of most of my building and give you my proposal." Mr. Angelo, until this moment, thought the shopkeeper's business was limited to the hobby shop itself. "I will say respectful things you need to know in order to make a decision and which you might not want anyone else to hear. Because you do not know me, you may want this young man to accompany us."

Mr. Angelo made a hand gesture to his bodyguard to come with them. Mr. Costa went to a section of the hobby shop which displayed a photovoltaic panel and pushed a button beside it. The panel slid aside, and an elevator door appeared. "I do not prefer the photovoltaic panels; they are very inefficient and need to store what little energy they make." He pushed the elevator button for the tenth floor. There were buttons with negative numbers as well, which did not go unnoticed by the visitors. The elevator had reached ten which was not a floor but the roof.

"Please observe the vast array of antennae. They serve various intelligence agencies to whom I lease space in this building. You notice the helipad as well. Many of my tenants have never been to this building through a street or garage entrance.

"My proposal to you is simple. I want to sell you my entire building on terms that will make you very rich. I will assign the long-term leases to you as well. I own this building outright, so there is no need for credit checks or outside financing. These tenants cherish privacy, secrecy and want no publicity. One condition of the sale would be that you give up other business enterprises, such as protecting small shop owners.

"Respectfully, a federal grand jury was to have been convened next Tuesday to indict a certain local businessman for RICO charges and extortion and racketeering. The U.S. Attorney has found from his investigators who rent here that all the businessmen who were being 'protected' have been reimbursed and have been provided actual insurance policies for their businesses, including for the entire time they were paying protection premiums. Each has willingly signed a non-prosecution statement saying they are very satisfied with the insurance purchased.

"The hobby shop, by the way, has been my hobby but is extremely profitable. It can go any direction a person wants. Some of its merchandise is supplied by enterprises located in other parts of the building. There is one floor dedicated to legitimate plants and one just for aquariums. There are contracts for me to supply all kinds of live fish. There is a fish 'library' along with a contract with three school districts to supply and maintain fish and tanks in classrooms. The employees there are employees of the hobby shop. There is a charter high school on the second floor. The solar energy floor does not produce energy but builds parts for solar projects modeled after the enormous farm, Solúcar, outside Seville, Spain— very efficient— mirrors."

No business was discussed during a pleasant supper, but Mr. Costa told of his father, a Greek shipping magnate, who left him his business skills. He did not mention money. He told of being a retired Navy seal trainer and then a commercial real estate broker.

Mrs. Costa made sure each person had enough to eat. She said she and her husband wanted to live in a one-story farmhouse they had bought in Tuscany and turn the business over to much younger people. Their granddaughter already had a horse being cared for there. Julia, who normally never spoke, said, "My horse's name is Macaroni. He is very gentle."

After a dessert of bread pudding and after some more conversation, Mrs. Costa said, "I hope you do not mind, but I tire very easily. I have a nurse in the next room who will assist me in retiring. Mr. and Mrs. Angelo and guests, this has been very enjoyable. I hope to see you often. Julia, please excuse yourself and say good night."

She complied as best she could with a huge smile for each person.

All the men stood as Mrs. Costa and Julia left the dining room. Mr. Angelo then asked his three employees to escort Mrs. Angelo to the car. He gave his wife a courtly kiss on the cheek and said, "I will be there very shortly."

The two men sat at the table, and nothing was said even after the door of the hobby shop closed.

Mr. Angelo was being offered an empire. He could see that. He was being offered an escape from his lifestyle of dodging other criminals and law enforcement, an escape from menacing his neighbors and employees and business associates. His wife could hold up her head, make friends, go to church without shame, and be in charge of charities and scholarships.

On the other hand, it would be very hard to live in a world where he was not feared. It would be admitting that his persona of intimidation was weak. He was speechless.

Finally, Mr. Costa, the man who was supposed to be his victim and afraid of him, spoke to Mr. Angelo and gently got right to the point. "I do not need an answer tonight or tomorrow or any time soon.

"You are the only person I want to own this building. With complete respect to you and your business abilities, if you accept my counterproposal, there is a staff of people with long-term contracts you can rely on, including accountants and a building manager who is responsible for all maintenance. All rents are automatically deposited, and all bills are reviewed by the building manager and submitted to you for payment. Even after making a monthly payment on the building to me, you would get a check every month after taxes have been withheld, which is vastly more than necessary for living expenses. There are even investment managers in the building.

"I do not know if this will help, but for me, in creating and running this building, I had to undergo a real attitude adjustment. People no longer fear me. It is sufficient if people always know I will do the right thing. That still scares people. I have been very happy. I will walk you to your car."

# LUKE AND JAN

Thomas sat at the deputy's desk in his father's office, concentrating on nothing but chemistry. He began his study session with strategy number one and strategy number two. One, relax, breathe in. *Spire* in Latin, to breathe. Every breath is an inspiration. Absorbing the gift of oxygen to replenish the trillions of cells at his command for a focused purpose. Strategy two, breathe out all carbon dioxide and depression. All depression is *expired* along with any sense of failure from prior difficulties. He was oblivious of the small town's rumors about the looming trial. The ruffians guarding the three roads into town he knew nothing about, although they were discussed throughout the town and in this very room. Even the sharp, sweet memories of his summer life-saving Rocky Mountain transformation were used only as motivation to concentrate more deeply until after his last makeup exam this afternoon. Strategy three: concentrate every thought to beat depression: swimming in an ice-cold lake feed by a glacier. Concentrate. Hiking in hail, snow, sleet, and rain all in one day up Meeker Peak. Concentrate. One step at a time. One sentence, one fact at a time. Strategies to concentrate on beating depression. Strategy four — defend all prior successes and picture your new success. Never back up, never lose a battle already won. I have won this battle before. I'll fight.

After this final makeup, he would be caught up with his classmates. Nothing would stop his concentration. Not even the growing noise outside the sheriff's office. One last review of three months of early morning and late-night studying. Well, almost nothing.

The oak door burst open and smashed into the deputy's desk while the deputy himself wrestled a young, shouting girl into the room and stopped before the sheriff. The girl tried to regain her composure by straightening her one-piece navy-blue jogging suit and checking her ponytail for damage.

Less than two hours ago, the deputy had been instructed to check that the ruffians guarding the roads were not doing anything illegal and then to patrol the town for anything out of the ordinary.

"Sheriff, this young lady was running at top speed right down the center of the street. I tried to hail her down, but she tried to evade me. I thought it was unusual."

"You have no right hold me. I have done nothing wrong."

"Thanks, Don. I'll take it from here. Young lady, there are some really rough men outside of town, and we are checking to see if you are in any danger.

"Were you being chased?"

"Just like a man. Blame the girl. It's always easier."

The sheriff looked at the girl more closely, surprised and confused, but repeated, "Were you being chased?"

"How dare you."

The agreement with his father was that he could study here but would never answer the phone or even speak while business was going on. Still facing the wall, Thomas raised his right hand, holding an index card containing three words.

"Your robot seems to have a question." *'Hmm. Cute robot.'*

The deputy took the card and handed it to the sheriff, who handed it to the girl. She read the three words, slowly turned red, and began to laugh beautifully. The deputy thought of sunshine breaking out after an unpleasant hail storm. Thomas was now thinking of a different type of chemistry.

"Oh, chased. Not chaste. I was always being chaste, but I was not being chased."

No reaction.

"No one was chasing me."

Some confusion remained on the faces of the sheriff and the deputy.

"May I have your name, please?"

Quoting a now obsolete court opinion that the legislature had rectified, she responded, "Since you had no right to stop me, I do not believe you are entitled to my name. I am entitled to ask you yours."

He looked at her carefully without correcting her legal opinion and without rancor said, "Where are my manners?

"My name is Sheriff David Hunter. This is my deputy, Don Williams, and my son, Thomas.

"I still need to know if you are safe."

Her face suddenly became unreadable again. "My 'protection' will be here in the morning. Meanwhile, good day, Sheriff, Deputy, robot." With a sideways glance in the direction of the deputy's desk, she swept out of the office and recommended running, her blonde ponytail and thoughts of "the robot" following close behind.

The next morning, a short woman stood at her cottage entrance, putting on her oversized parka the only way she could. She put on the sleeves first as if she were diving. Then she stood up straight, and gravity pulled the heavy, oversized jacket into place. She was so short the parka looked like a trench coat. She would explain the injury to her arm, but the explanation involved the last years of World War II and took some time.

She had lived over ninety-three adventurous years, and the next few days would hold no less adventure. She was up early as always, preparing to go to daily mass in the small town's Catholic church.

Without formal education beyond primary school in a small French village and some English acquired as an au pair in England before the war, Nanette nonetheless became very talented through years of study and practice in many areas. Farming, sewing, cooking, canning, making candles and soap, nothing surprised the townspeople about her. Her apricot brandy was powerful and discussed with reverence. The one gallon recycled glass mayonnaise jars from the town restaurant contained the fermenting apricots. Two were sufficient even for a drinker.

She had designed and overseen the construction of her small home. Cabinets for smoking meat were built into the sides of the chimney. She had a simple pulley on a beam just past the edge of her porch. When the town hunters brought her game, they would help her hoist it so she could dress the animal. Nothing was wasted. The hide was tanned, and the bone ground into meal for what had become the town's garden. Everything edible was neatly packaged, and most was returned to the hunters' families with some for her. Her apprentices did most of that now.

The town's children called her grandmother and remembered watching as she gently instructed the men during her first autumn to scrape all the soil off the garden site into a mound at one end and bring the muck from their barns to spread as the base for the winter garden. The topsoil was then spread back in place. The decaying compost of manure and straw beneath would prevent the garden from freezing and would provide ample winter vegetables for everyone. The first year the men did as she asked in her quaint, thick French accent just to humor her, but after the first year, it became a profitable town tradition.

It was never surprising when a child returned home from a visit to Nanette with instructions of how to make soap or candles or a particular meal with the necessary ingredients included.

The glass storm door was the one part of her cottage she had not chosen. She had deferred to the wisdom of the local builders and was again today very pleased she had. She stood back from the door so that her breath would not fog the glass and studied her small kingdom in the clear, cold silence. Snow covered the small New England town, excluding the garden which stretched from her cottage to the back of the courthouse. No snow covered the garden. Occasional wisps of steam escaping from the garden gave evidence of the heat and power of the compost underneath.

The pre-dawn sun just beyond the horizon was highlighting the very few clouds in the sky. Nanette, of course, thought of the artist Caravaggio and how he made light appear to be coming from inside an object. The clouds appeared on fire from their insides.

Glancing at a brilliant dot in the high distance, she watched it grow to become a plane. It was not at all loud. It circled twice and began an approach toward the courthouse and her cottage. Nanette thought she could see a tiny object leave the plane, then saw a parachute deploy which eventually carried two figures or maybe three toward the courthouse, eventually depositing them behind a parapet on the courthouse roof just beyond her garden. So very close. The pilot circled once more, probably to see that the parachute had hit its target and then disappeared also.

"Deja vu!"

Her startled remark was loud enough to disturb the old yellow lab napping before the fireplace. Suddenly she flashed back to her French village the morning of the Normandy Invasion. The town's mayor summoned her because she spoke some limited English from her time in England. She was asked to interpret for the huge, rough soldier parachutists who were surrounding the mayor. Everyone in the town was terrified. The mayor indicated by sign language and near gibberish that Nanette could speak some English. He indicated they should talk to her with both his hands thrust toward her, his palms up.

"Howdy, ma'am. We're here to liberate y'all's town."

She closed her eyes, praying fervently to God that these men did not speak French, and addressed the mayor in a whisper, "Don't trust them. They must be German. Nobody speaks English like that."

One of the men understood enough of what she said. "Ma'am, we're army airborne rangers from Texas. We all talk like this."

She was invited that very day to visit Texas to see for herself. Years after the war, she did exactly that and confirmed that some people do speak like her town's liberators.

Her flashback over, there was no evidence of what she had seen. But she watched the top of the courthouse and saw something thrown over the parapet. Then one small figure began to climb down a rope ladder, followed by another small figure. The beige rope blended with the rear wall of the courthouse, and when the two figures got to the ground and scurried around the corner of the building, there was no evidence that they had ever been there. She thought, *"But, perhaps there were three."*

Grandmother Nanette pondered these things as she let the dog out briefly and again on her way to St. Joseph's Chapel, two blocks past the front of the courthouse.

Meanwhile, two of the young parachutists had decided that the warmest place in town would be in the highest part of the church they had seen while landing. They went around the right side of the courthouse, past the side of the snowy town square, past the sheriff's office, into the chapel's vestibule, and up the stairs to the loft, all without anyone else seeing them.

The church was built of fieldstone and kept beautifully simple. All the wood for the rafters, the pews, the altar, and the carved crucifix suspended above it came from the forests surrounding the town. The stones were donated by farmers glad to have them out of their fields. The main floor was slate. Townspeople of every religion did the construction.

From their dark perch in the choir loft, they saw the elderly priest preparing his church for the daily mass. They could only see over the rail when they stood. Thankfully, he turned on the heat which reached them first while the handful of faithful came in and divested themselves of their outermost winter gear in stages as the small church became warmer.

The boys watched a short elderly lady who rocked precariously from side to side as she slowly proceeded up the center aisle to the front pew, left side. She nodded humbly toward the tabernacle as she was incapable of genuflecting. She slid off her parka and removed her grey scarf, which matched her very straight hair. She adjusted her hair comb and then replaced her scarf which used to be required in church.

They whispered in Dutch when they spoke at all. Most of their communication was intuitive, done with nods and looks and facial expressions. They had been up all night. They were sleepy, and the choir loft was now warm. They heard parts of the sermon. Luke spoke English and had taught some to his brother.

Down below, in the front pew, Nanette thought to herself that she could have given the sermon. Once again, the priest lamented that so few people came to mass and that no one sang.

He finished with the same challenge as always. "At the end of Mass, I will sing the thousand-year-old Latin conclusion in Gregorian chant, 'Ite, missa est.' And who will sing that beautiful response, 'Deo Gratias?' The day someone does, I will contact the bishop and tell him my work is done. Perhaps he will send you some young handsome, humorous priest who can draw large crowds.

Upstairs, Jan thought he understood the English words and thought it odd. Back home in Europe, they sang the mass daily with their classmates and on special occasions in Latin. Not to sing would be strange.

They had dozed off a little, but when the old priest began to sing in a surprisingly strong voice, the twins stood in the dark choir loft. The old man's arms were outstretched, and he prepared for a dramatic pause to emphasize the silence he was expecting. Instead, the children's voices softly filled the church with their angelic response, and the priest gripped the altar to prevent himself from falling.

Jan whispered, "Our work here is done. Did you see the priest? He seemed very surprised. I am sure he was pleased."

They left the chapel without being seen.

"Deputy, where did that girl go when she left yesterday?"

"Ran straight down the street and out of sight."

"If you see her, invite her back. Oddly enough, her father wants her. Also, have you ever heard of anyone around here named Chippendale? The father suspects that that is who has his daughter."

"No, I don't know, but there is a club in Bath with dancing. Or, I could check the furniture store."

"Funny. There are a lot of peculiar things going on. Somehow, I think they are all connected to the trial. The priest tried to file a complaint about criminal trespass at the church. Imagine. Says a stranger sang at the end of services this morning, says it might have been a professional recording. One of the parishioners said it was two angels. The priest says it is the devil undermining him with local help.

"Please go out and check on our three groups of "inspectors." They are trying to prevent any witnesses from coming into town. I ran plates for all three cars— all registered to a restaurant in Bath owned by the father of the defendant."

The phone rang. "Sheriff's office. Deputy Williams. Yes, sir. I got it. I understand. We'll look into it. Thank you, Bill."

The sheriff's look was a question.

"Bill Hardy. Said someone got into his service station restroom and cleaned it. Customers are laughing at him, and he's sore."

"Men's or women?"

"Men's."

The sheriff sat and pondered for a few minutes after the deputy left. He replayed a message from Homeland Security. He took a fresh yellow notepad and put the date and time at the top, and wrote under those the name and phone number from the message. Then he dialed and asked for the name on his notepad and identified himself. For the next ten minutes, he listened. Three times the special agent asked, "Are you still there?" Each time, "Yes, sir. I am listening very closely."

As the notes on the yellow pad would very accurately reflect, the special agent had received a call from a most angry U.S. Army colonel stationed at the Hague who had just left the office of his commander. The commander had received a message sent by Morse code picked up by their military satellite saying the same as what the sheriff had listened to earlier before returning this call. "Your daughter is safe. Love. Chippendale."

The commander had sent out a base-wide message ordering anyone who knew about a missing daughter or Chippendale to see him immediately.

First came the colonel. He was under orders to return to the States within a week. Commercial plane tickets were on his desk at home, but, as usual, he had not told his very independent daughter. She had apparently seen and taken her ticket and booked an earlier flight.

The special agent said she was picked up upon arrival at Brunswick by a privately owned vehicle and taken very near the sheriff's town. The driver was identified, located, and interviewed. He said some tough men were blocking the road a good distance ahead, so she took a large backpack and disappeared into a snowy forest after telling him she had left a very angry man in Europe. That turned out to be misleading but true.

The commander's second visitor was a very squared-away sergeant who said, "Sir, I suspect the commander is looking for Chip and Dale, nicknames for two boys with a relative doing special forces training with some of the European armies. The mother is dead, and the father teaches driver's education to our military dependents in anticipation of their returning to the States. They follow all soldiers' training, mostly undetected, and practice stealth and martial arts between themselves."

The special homeland security agent concluded his call with the sheriff by saying, "The colonel knows nothing about 'Chip and Dale.' He seems volatile, so I will leave him to you. I gave him your number."

"Thank you, special agent. Goodbye."

Nanette returned to her cottage and to her dog. She was still enjoying the end of mass and still reflecting on what she had seen before dawn. *"Flying angels…. Singing angels."*

Almost everyone in the town loved Nanette. But there were two children, ignorant and uneducated so far, who lived outside the town. The boy and his younger sister would pass behind Nanette's cottage, between the cottage and the river, on their way to school and its free breakfast. From time to time, they would throw rocks onto her metal roof, which slanted to the back so steeply that no snow stayed on it. If she were outside, they would hurl insults at her because she was foreign and different and rocked from side to side when she walked.

This day they threw rocks at the roof and then ran toward the river covered with a thin layer of ice. The small girl got too close to the steep riverbank and fell down the bank and through the ice. Her shill cries were joined by her brother's shouts for help.

Great sadness came over Nanette. Duty called. She opened the storm door and told her last, her most precious, her only companion, "Go, Annie. Go save the child."

Yellow Labs are natural water dogs, but Annie was not young and was heavy. Nanette heard her splash and then more screaming and shouting. She did not want to become ninety-four alone. Minutes went by unnoticed. She could hear the boy and the girl talking loudly, then their voices faded. They were probably running, probably back home. She thought the steep riverbank was too much for Annie. She was ready never to move again. Her dog did not bark or bang on the storm door. There was silence.

Finally, there came a small knocking. Expecting the worst news, she went to her storm door. Two boys with tennis ball haircuts were dripping wet and freezing and helping her beautiful Annie stand between them. Annie weakly licked their hands.

She put them in front of the fireplace after directing Jan to put on another log from the firewood recess beside the chimney and Luke to haul beautiful down comforters from a large blanket box.

She had them put blankets down first, then more on top. She surprised them when she said, "Shoes" first in English than in French. She stuffed the shoes with newspaper and put them near the fire. She ordered them to turn over their pants and shirts for drying after they were under the covers with Annie in the middle. Their drenched jackets from the front porch were retrieved and carefully dried as well.

The adventurers slept like logs as the different shirts and jackets were drying near the fire. A venison stew bubbled on as the heroic trio slept into the afternoon. Finally, the dog became restless.

————•————

The district attorney's third call of the day to the sheriff began abruptly, even for him. "Trial begins in the morning, and I am missing two witnesses. A boy is charged with last summer's sexual contact with a local sixteen-year-old. The victim's mother says her daughter will not talk except to say two boys from Harlem saw everything. They may show, or they may not. The defendant's father is connected. He will prevent them from testifying or even appearing if he can. The best evidence I have that they haven't found the boys is that his muscle is still guarding the three roads. That is why I have asked you to leave them in place until the trial."

"The only two black people in the town are the judge's clerk and her son, my deputy. I'd ask again if they knew of any visitors from Harlem last summer."

The Lab licked the boys until they could not ignore her. Luke, laughing, said, "You have to stop."

Nanette was constantly tending the clothes so they would dry and not scorch. Turning, she asked, "So, you speak English?"

"Only me. I am Luke. This is my brother, Jan. He speaks Dutch, French, and Spanish."

"Je Suis Jan."

"Every summer, we go to the language camp in Bath to learn a new language. The first time a student speaks any language he is not learning, he is warned. The second time he is sent home."

Jan told her in French how the dog pulled the girl to the side of the river with her wrist clamped in the Lab's mouth. She could not get the girl up the embankment, so we jumped in and delivered the girl to her brother and then lifted her together," he said smiling at the dog."

Luke told her, also in French, that they were tardy and had to find a friend from Europe. They had agreed to meet her today.

Nanette told them, also in French, that the sheriff's deputy said there were very bad men guarding the roads into town, looking for witnesses. The boys exchanged quick, nervous looks.

"We know. We met some of them. They are looking for black children from Harlem who might be witnesses.

"They do not know they are looking for us. We are from the first Harlem in the Netherlands. Our cousin helped us arrive at the courthouse to stay away from the bad men. We practice parachutes with our cousin every summer when language school is out. This time he used only one parachute to be certain we met the courthouse roof."

The boys put on their now toasty warm clothes while Nanette took Annie outside. After a meal of stew, they told Nanette, "We will be back, but now we have to find our friend, Julia. She will be camping in the snow outside of town. Our cousin helped us send a Morse message for her father to receive so he would know she was safe. We do not want him discommoded."

Thomas had successfully finished his credit by exam and was free. Free from studying and free from the depression which had nearly destroyed his life. The summer strategies he had learned were now his constant companions. He knew it was not enough not to be depressed. Otherwise, he was waiting around to be depressed again. His doctor taught him angst is normal, but if he let it keep coming back—boomerangst. He was a most humorous doctor. Strategy four was to set the next goal and then go back to strategies one, two, and three.

Walking down the town's "most main street," as the locals called it, he heard someone calling,

"Young man… young man."

Thomas turned, expecting to find an elderly person calling him. Instead, he saw two identical boys with short, blonde haircuts hidden from the street between two buildings.

"Yes?"

"We are looking for a girl."

"I think you should each be looking for a girl. One girl for two boys is not enough."

Jan said in Spanish, "He looked normal."

Luke said, "We need to find our friend. She is not from here. She needs our help. She is camping in the snow close to this town. She has a tail like a pony." Even Jan did not think that sounded right.

"I understand. Blonde. You are her protectors. I can help you. As soon as I ask my father one question, I will know where she is. Stay here, please."

Jan whispered in French, "We are getting closer. He sounds like he is crazy, but now I think he may help us."

Minutes later, the sheriff spoke again with the special agent from Homeland Security, who told him precisely where the driver said he had left the girl and her backpack. The son took the information and returned to the main street.

"I can take you very close to where she must be, but we have to stay away from some very bad men."

"Yes, we know this. My cousin and I tried to enter the town normally, but we met very ugly men. My cousin tried another road with my brother with more bad men."

The small hike through deep snow took nearly half an hour because they had to stay off the road and watch for trouble. Small footprints in deep snow led them to a dome tent and the blonde runner from yesterday.

Julia!"

"Luke, Jan. Wow. You brought the robot."

"She has only been back in America one day, and she has lost her mind."

"My father wants to talk to you. He will keep all of you safe." The camp gear was packed and carried through the woods. Thomas and the girl spoke quietly.

"Why did you run away from your father?"

"I just left early. He has been reassigned to the States at a base nearby, but he never tells me about us moving until he is ready to board the plane. I am sixteen and should be treated with some respect. Besides, I knew Jan and Luke were going to be in this town because they told me they would testify or die trying. They are my protection."

The four arrived at the sheriff's office, but it was empty. Thomas went to find his father, and Julia went to freshen up.

Two minutes later, the phone on the sheriff's desk rang. Jan proved why he needed English lessons. "Sheriff."

"This is Colonel Millis. I will be there in one week, and I want to know what anybody in your little town is doing to find Julia, my daughter." Many unrepeatable words followed.

"Your daughter is safe. Be comfortable."

"Comfortable. Comfortable. Is this Chippendale as in 'Love, Chippendale'?"

"Je Suis Chip."

"Love, Love. If you are sleeping with my daughter, I will kill you, sheriff or no sheriff."

"Who can sleep? She talks always."

The Colonel had apparently disconnected with a bang. Julia had returned. "Who was that?"

"Father. Your father. I cannot fall asleep in front of you, or he will kill me. I am only twelve. I... must... sleep."

"I will pay for your English lessons next summer even if I have to get a job." Then to Luke, "When does your cousin get to town?"

"Oh, he is here. He will be in the place very early tomorrow morning. We, indicating Jan and himself, will be at the place very early, too, so no one sees us."

"Do they know you are here?"

"The bad men are looking everywhere but do not know they are looking for us. They look for Black boys from Harlem."

Nanette watched for the boys. She saw an older, larger version of them come out of the woods and go directly to the rear wall of the courthouse. He climbed the rope ladder and disappeared onto the roof.

The uneducated boy and girl came to the storm door with their mother. Her daughter had told her that two boys and the vicious dog had pushed her into the water and that her brother had saved her. "You will be hearing from my attorney." They wouldn't come in.

Nanette told her, "A mother's heart knows what her ears never heard. If children threw rocks at my roof and ran toward the river, and one of them fell in, that could have been terrible. If they go home and the girl thinks, 'My clothes are wet, we are not at school, my mother will be angry. I will tell her a story, and my brother will help me.' The riverbank is steep, and he would have to jump in to save her. If he saved her, he would be very wet when he went home. How did he arrive, madam, I ask you? Dry or wet?"

"I did not pay attention to my son because my daughter nearly drowned." She looked at her children appraisingly, especially at her son, and with her understanding came true anger. The defeated mother finally said, "I have no proof of what happened, so I will not waste my money on an attorney."

"Madam, I wish you a life as long as mine, and for the rest of my life, I will be your friend. Please come and visit me and bring your children. When it is summer, they can help in the garden. Please take some vegetables and smoked meat."

———•———

The boys were at the sheriff's office when Thomas returned. They asked him permission to turn Julia over to the sheriff for her protection. "She will be safer away from us tomorrow. And she is too…saucy for us." That earned a beautiful smile from her.

Speaking to Julia, "That's perfect. My father wants you to stay at our house with my aunt and my father, and me, for now."

The boys returned to Nanette's cottage at dark and told her in a barrage of different languages how their cousin, the parachutist, had first encountered the men at the edge of town. They had guns. "We are looking for a couple of Black punks." One of the thugs rubbed his thumb down the cousin's face as if he might have disguised himself with white paint. "Lucky for you." Each entranceway was checked and also guarded. The thugs had never seen the twins together, so they did not grow suspicious of them.

They recounted to Nanette their father's speech at the breakfast table as they prepared to leave home. "You are to ride in the military transport plane.

You have permission. In my time, you had to pay a dollar each if you had to use a parachute, but I am sure you will never need a parachute.

"You will tell the judge what you saw last summer. I have never spoken to you about that, and you can truthfully say so. You will say that your cousin saw the article about the trial asking the two witnesses to come forward.

"Your mother and brother are looking over you and will keep you safe.

"One last thing. Do not make fun of the Americans. You are there to tell the truth in court and make friends. If you get a chance, go to church. Nothing can go wrong in church."

"Yes, father."

They told how, on each attempt to come into town, their cousin only let one ride with him because the thugs were looking for two boys. "Our cousin spends part of the year in Europe in some sort of training and spends summers here. We live with him and learn language most of the summer. We practice martial arts and parachuting."

It was late, and they ate thick, smoked venison sandwiches and had an apricot each for dessert which took their breath away.

———•———

Thomas and his aunt sat on the sofa facing Julia in a recliner across the coffee table.

Thomas talked about his summer— great grueling hikes in the Rocky Mountains, calf muscles screaming, motivating troubled children from all over the Midwest, and sometimes just keeping up with the ones that were motivated. He spoke of the camaraderie of the camp staff and of some of the amazing children.

Then he decided to put the story in order. "Last spring, my mother left us. I failed every single class. I had been a star athlete and a top student with hopes of a college scholarship. I quit speaking, eating, even bathing. I stunk. I would not leave my room. I was diagnosed with extreme depression, and my father was afraid for my life. I was sent to a clinic in Evergreen, Colorado, for a long-term commitment. As teenagers, the doctor and my father had been counselors at a camp near Roosevelt National Park and became trusted friends for life.

"The doctor gave me two, two-hour sessions per day. He is the most infuriating, motivating person I have ever met. The first day he told me, 'I will teach you strategies. Use them or reject them.'

"At the beginning of the second week, I went to my morning session. He said, 'Stay locked up here all summer or be a counselor at a camp for children nearly as nutty as you. I have taught you four ways to handle your problem. You are about to use them or not. I'm leaving in ten minutes—make up your mind. If you're coming, bring your stuff.'

"Boulder fields to cross, steep trails through the pines, then the timberline with grass and shrubs replacing the trees, arriving at midsummer snowfields exhausted and suddenly totally but briefly reinvigorated by the cold from the snow, chocolate bars for the children for the last push to the summit always before noon because of the afternoon lightning. Spoiled children who transformed faster than I did. My therapist worked there as the head counselor. He hiked and camped and ate with us. Engage. Engage. Engage. Confrontation and inclusiveness at the same time. First names or nicknames only. Even the doctor, John.

"The very angry old man who built the huge lodge years ago stayed on as a handyman in his cottage. His dog, a Chow, would attack cars coming onto the camp property, barking ferociously, pushing itself off the hood, and disappearing only to jump again against the hood. It finally got injured. Its back legs would not work. After a week of carrying the dog, the old man carried the dog into the woods with his rifle strapped on his back. That dog really understood his choices. While the old man was telling that story at the campfire one night, John made eye contact with me across the fire and then tilted his head toward the storyteller as if I should understand his story and my own choice. He meant it to be a joke, but I was furious at the comparison. Suddenly I was sobbing out of true self-compassion, uncontrollably sobbing. I had not even realized that he had led me away from the fire and the campers. I finally got my breath and said, 'She just left us… It was not my fault.'"

By the time his father got home, he was talked out. His father said state troopers had been brought in because if the Black children found a way into town to testify, they would be in serious danger because the case was against a powerful man's son. His deputy was assigned to be the court bailiff for more security.

Thomas told his father about who the witnesses actually were. The father said he would patrol the town tomorrow as if searching for the nonexistent Black witnesses.

The next morning the sheriff and deputy searched the town and surprisingly could not find them. The rough men from the roadblocks had moved into town and were searching, too.

Nanette was hanging her quilts to air on a long clothesline. Two men approached.

"We're looking for two Black boys from Harlem," one said, staring at her, expecting an answer.

"I have not seen any Black children from Harlem. How did you do in history and geography?"

"Crazy old woman. She doesn't know anything."

"Lonely," the other said.

*"Not lately,"* she thought.

No one looked in the courtroom. And especially, no one looked in the witness box. The witness box was attached to the judge's bench on his left. It had a solid wooden front and a swinging gate on the side away from the judge's bench for access. The boys sat on the floor of the witness box with their backs against the solid wooden front. They heard the courtroom door being unlocked, and they could hear the townspeople shuffling in and slowly filling the room. The buzz reminded Luke of when their father had received a shipment of bees, and the instructions said to "paint" the screen sides of the container with a new brush with sugar water.

Of course, almost everyone was present. The courtroom held more people than anywhere else in town except the high school gym or possibly the church, but according to the priest, they would probably never know. The bishop sat in the back row with the unhappy priest on his right and Thomas and Julia on his left. The bishop was *not* exactly here for the trial.

A very aggressive district attorney sat at the council table to the right directly in front of the witness box with hopes that this case could catapult him to a job in the capital.

The bristling defense attorney, displaying a confidence he may or may not have possessed, occupied the other table. He was pretending to confer with the seventeen-year-old defendant while mostly trying to do the will of the young man's father.

The bailiff called, "All rise. District Court for this County and State is now in session, the Honorable Judge Robert Shepherd presiding." From that moment, anyone else who thought he owned the courtroom began to understand most clearly who was in charge.

As the judge faced the people, he saw the district attorney on his left, alone, and the defense attorney and his client at the table on his right.

"Be seated, please."

The judge asked the district attorney, "Is the State ready to proceed to trial?"

"The State is ready, your Honor."

The district attorney knew the defense would ask for a jury trial, which allowed him to posture and insist he was ready with his entire case, but he had two flaws in his case as it stood today. The victim's mother was vocal about the brutality of this crime, but the victim was not. In fact, the daughter refused to testify, saying that nothing had happened, that two boys from Harlem were witnesses. The mother had added "Black" to her daughter's description. She thought, "Who else comes from Harlem?" The second flaw in his case was that the only two Black people in the courtroom were the clerk and the bailiff, mother and son. Despite his efforts, the two witnesses identified by the vociferous mother as two Black children from Harlem were nowhere to be seen today. He was very confident they would be located and forced to testify at the jury trial a month from now.

"Is the defense ready to proceed?"

The defense attorney stood and slowly turned, scanning the courtroom. He even saw the top of the blonde head of one of the brothers in the witness box but dismissed him as he was not Black. He saw no Black children. He was a courtroom strategist, a veteran. The courtroom was silent, everyone expecting demand for a jury trial. The judge made eye contact with the clerk, which meant to bring his trial calendar.

"The defense waives a jury trial and requests that we proceed immediately. We place ourselves in this Court's just hands." He had never even seen the judge before.

The courtroom again sounded like a very active beehive. The judge did not bang his gavel or order the bailiff to call for an order. He simply allowed the buzz to abate while in his mind he cancelled the jury trial and rearranged his lunch plans.

The district attorney's next move was not surprising to the judge or the defense attorney. "Your Honor, may we approach the bench." Still hopeful of salvaging his ambitions, the district attorney wanted only the judge and opposing counsel to hear him admit how he had colossally miscalculated. The defense attorney was still wary. He understood the prosecutor's dilemma and wanted it to remain a dilemma.

"Your Honor, the State is ready, of course. The State can begin with background witnesses and then the victim's mother. Two of my witnesses are delayed, and there might be too long an interruption before I call them. If the court would allow a continuance until next week for the presentation of the State's entire case, I could guarantee no further interruptions once my witnesses from Harlem arrive."

From the witness box, Jan said in a loud voice, "Harlem?"

The judge stood in order to see the source of this question. He did not speak. He looked at both boys and understood.

Luke stood. Then Jan. The crowd was mesmerized.

"Fee are fitnesses from Harlem." Luke was embarrassed and his face very red, but he was determined to speak English without a further accent.

The district attorney hated them instantly. A case that could propel him from this small county to the capital, and he was totally unprepared. He would still win, and he still hated them.

The defense attorney hated them. Seconds ago, victory, gratitude, and a fat check from his client's father were his. These two were eyewitnesses. They evaded the paid ruffians of the client's father and for all he knew their testimony could put his biggest client's son away for years. He had little chance to charm, intimidate, or bribe them here in open court. Worse, he had openly waived a jury trial because nobody here knew enough history or geography.

"Your Honor, The State requests a few days' continuances in order to properly investigate what these two young men might know and present it to the court."

"Denied."

"Your Honor, normally the defense would not join in the State's request for more time to develop the facts of a case, but here the defense…."

"Denied. Step away from the bench." All this had taken place at the bench, but now the judge spoke so that everyone present could hear, "Mr. Prosecutor, read the charge."

The district attorney did so.

"How does the defendant plead?"

The defendant stood before the defense attorney could rise. In fact, he put his hand on the defense attorney's shoulder to prevent him from rising, "I am not guilty, Your Honor."

The judge noted that the young man had intentionally separated himself from the defense attorney and from his father's power. The judge saw the defendant's mother directly behind the defendant sit up straighter, displaying pride in her son and displaying her own humble dignity.

"Very well. Do you still waive a jury trial?"

With his hand still on the not-happy defense attorney's shoulder, "Yes, Your Honor, I do."

Not everything of consequence that happens during a trial is said out loud. The defendant, named Nicolas, looked humbly and frankly at the two boys still standing in the witness box. He appeared most grateful for their presence. The boys returned his glance and appeared calm about him.

"Your Honor, I would like to call my first witness, the victim's mother." He was hoping to stall until the noon hour and its recess to be able to work privately with the boys and their testimony.

"Your Honor, I object to anyone being called 'the victim's mother.' "There is no presumption that any crime has been committed or that there is a victim."

"Sustained. Approach."

The prosecutor and the defense attorney were back at the bench. "I would like to ask a favor of both of you."

A day of more surprises. When a judge "asks" for something.

"Many people have been searching for these two," glancing at the witness box. Then his eyes rested on the district attorney. "These children are under this court's protection. If they testify now, the danger to them is not eliminated but is greatly reduced. I would like them called first and then for them to remain in the courtroom, in my view."

"Yes, your honor."

Back at his table, the district attorney announced that he would call his first witnesses, the young men already in the witness box.

The judge asked the young men to remain standing so that they could be seen. "I will also remain standing so that I can see you, too." He asked the defense attorney to move his table over so that both tables were side by side directly in front of the witness box. This placed Nicolas really close to the seething district attorney. Nicolas was comfortable with the arrangement, and the district attorney was really not.

Even administering the oaths was interesting. "Do you know what it means to tell the truth?"

"Yes, your honor, we learn the truth at home and school and church. Our word kirk is the word for church. Jan understood and nodded assent.

"Yes, speaking of kirk or church… here…yesterday?"

"We were in the top of the church. I slept a little. My brother, Jan," (small bow from Jan). "His English is not ready, said the priest invited people to sing the last prayer at mass. We helped him. He seemed very surprised. We think he was pleased."

The judge, having heard a different version, kept a straight face.

"I am Luke. Jan speaks English only a small amount. Our father says Jan thinks hominy grits is a question. When we need English, I speak. When we need Spanish, Jan speaks. But we were arrested in Mexico once for 'invasion of the sovereignty of the language of Mexico.' "He repeated the charge against them very slowly and deliberately. "The officer was very young and said Jan was attacking his country's language and that we were a national threat. We think he did not like us and invented that law. Next summer Jan will learn English like me."

The judge looked over the packed courtroom to indicate this would be a poor time to laugh.

The district attorney scribbled questions as fast as he could and tried to hide them from Nicolas beside him, who was paying no attention to the district attorney.

The defense asked permission "to take the witnesses on void dire to ascertain their qualifications and truthfulness."

"I will allow it."

"Please be precise with your answers. Do you each understand? Names?"

"Jan Brakhuis"

"Luke Brakhuis."

"Ages?"

Luke allowed Jan to answer in Dutch and then translated.

"Twelve…each." The judge might have thought this last word was a smart remark but let it slide.

"How did you get here?"

"Airplane."

"Well, of course, by plane from Europe. How did you get to this town?"

"Airplane."

"Would it interest you to know that this town does not have an airport?"

Both boys nodded. Both understood or thought they did. Jan spoke, then Luke, both completely missing the angry defense attorney's sarcasm and implied accusation of their dishonesty. "We agree. That is interesting. It made the landing (hesitation and then agreement between the two) very difficult."

Probably no one in the courtroom could have been paid any amount to leave. Not the bishop or the priest, not Thomas or Julia, and not Nanette in the front row. The judge has a duty to protect witnesses from abuse but cannot protect them from the consequences of possible perjury.

The defense attorney more or less asked permission before demolishing these witnesses.

"May I continue, Your Honor?"

"Continue."

"Where did you land?"

Each pointed up with his index finger.

With dripping sarcasm, "Can you tell us how you landed on the roof of this building?"

The boys looked for words first but then looked at each other as if understanding each other without words. Together they lifted the parachute from the floor of the witness box and held it up.

The judge thoroughly enjoyed saying, "Let the record reflect that the witnesses have held up a white parachute."

"We had a guide to help us meet the roof. It is a directional parachute."

The defense attorney tried to act as if this were all very boring. "I reserve the remainder of my questions for cross-examination."

The district attorney was going to be very circumspect with his questions. The boys' credibility was very great, but he still hated them. They were dangerous. The seasoned defense attorney had just proven that by relearning the law school adage, "Never ask a question if you do not know the answer. "Why by airplane?"

"Luke let Jan talk and then said, "Each road had bad men looking for two boys from Harlem. We thought one of them might remember his geography class from school."

"Would the Court please instruct the witnesses to refrain from sarcasm?"

"No."

'Ouch.' "Why did you come?"

"To tell the truth," Luke spoke alone, but Jan nodded.

"You must be very brave to testify against a young man with such a powerful family."

With feigned outrage, the defense attorney was on his feet. "I object to the slanderous characterization of my client's family."

"Overruled." To the witnesses, "You may answer the question if you think there was a question."

Jan spoke, then Luke translated, "We are not brave. We are not afraid. We came to tell the truth. We are not here to testify against the young man" (pointing at Nicolas, less than fifteen feet away). "We saw everything with the young man" (Jan pointed at Nicolas, then Luke pointed at Nicolas) "and with the young woman." (Jan pointed her out, and then Luke pointed at her). Luke added, "Our father told us to tell the truth and to tell you that he has never asked us about what to say."

"Did he tell you anything else?"

"Do not make fun of the Americans. We are here to make friends and to tell the truth."

"Anything else?"

"Yes. Go to church if we can. Nothing can go wrong in church."

A man in the back row, a bishop, said to the man beside him, the priest, "That's my favorite part so far."

"I will pass the witnesses but will get to what they saw on the date in question upon my redirect."

There was a pause before the defense attorney began. He had seriously miscalculated and had just been burnt by children. He was torn between attacking the witnesses and believing his young client's story of actual innocence. His instinct for cynicism won.

"Isn't it a fact that the district attorney has agreed not to charge you with breaking into a service station in exchange for your testimony?"

A long discussion between Luke and Jan in different languages. More discussion. Finally, Luke said, "No."

"Noooo?" One syllable packed with venom and menace.

"After kirk, church, we had to use the services and did not want to disrespect this town." Jan piped in and told Luke he thought it was important to tell that their cousin gave them strong vitamins that made them urinate what looked like yellow traffic paint, and they wanted to use proper facilities.

The judge said, "Let's only talk about whether you went into the service station."

The boys were beginning to suspect the judge spoke Dutch.

"We used my library card to slide behind the latch and went inside to use the room for men. In trade, we repaired the toilet and cleaned the floor and walls as high as we could feel, reach. Then we washed and left." (Jan spoke only to his brother.) "Also, my brother says since we are tired, we would like to tell the truth now." The audience was certainly ready, even if the attorneys were not. The district attorney asked the judge to allow the boys to testify in the narrative form like a person simply telling a story. This is allowed when the witness is young or when language is a barrier.

"Objection. I request that they be made to testify by question and answer."

"Overruled. Tell your brother to speak with pauses so that you can interpret. If you have trouble saying something in English, say so, and we will all come to some agreement. All of this was being told to Jan when the defense attorney stood and asked the judge with what sounded like respect, "Your Honor, I understand your ruling and, of course, respect it. This case concerns allegations of sexual activity. Would the court consider asking the witnesses if they know what sex is?"

"That is a good suggestion. Turning to his left, "Do you both know what sex is?"

After a long chat in the witness box, Luke answered. "Yes, Jan wants you to know we know what sex is and what is not sex. Jan wants you to know we 'have been to Amsterdam', which means we know, we have seen everything. Jan was at first so disgusted with how people are created that he did not want to talk to our parents for two weeks. He could not decide which one he did not want to talk to first." There was a tugging on Luke's shirt sleeve. Jan was not satisfied with this portrayal as final. "Thank you. Jan wants you to know, not really wants, but he thinks you should know that he now approves and thinks it is a good idea."

No one spoke, so Luke interpreted during the pauses. "We were in this Maine state visiting a certain cousin for the summer learning more languages.

He brought us to your lake for the Independence Celebration. That is the only rest that the school allows.

"We hiked around the lake but higher than the trail through the trees. We stopped to rest at a big rock like a table. We saw many people from our view."

"This boy and this girl were sitting on a bench below us next to the trail, looking to the lake and to each other." They indicated Nicolas and the alleged victim by each pointing at them again.

The narrative and the interpretation were satisfactory so far. Too satisfactory for the defense attorney. He was afraid of what might come next and that it would be too late to object. He wanted a way to derail the testimony.

"Our father teaches driver's education in Harlem and sometimes in the military schools. He tells his students and us that two physical objects cannot use the same space...." Faltering.

"Occupy."

"Cannot occupy the same space at the same time."

"Your honor, I am requesting a recess. What relevance can this driving school and sitting on a big rock have to do with the charges? It is clear they need a rest."

"We think it shows they never took our father's class." The audience laughed without objection from the court.

"Overruled. I am asking you both just tell me what you saw."

"They were very close to each other. We thought they were expecting more people to come to sit on the bench with them." There was more buzz in the courtroom.

"They got off the bench and went behind small bushes and took off most of their clothes." The room got very silent.

"They were behind different bushes. They were wearing swimming apparatus."

"Do you mean swimming apparel?"

"Yes, sir, Judge. Thank you. Swimming clothes. We sat on the rock and watched everyone swim. Many people. When they came out of the water, they went to their own bushes to regain their clothes. No sex.

"That mother came and started screaming. She saw them without all the clothes, and the young woman asked her to stop screaming. The mother screamed that her daughter had been bothered...mo....."

"Molested?"

"Yes. That was her word."

The defense attorney had never won like this. He was speechless.

Not the district attorney. He was furious.

"That's it? That's it? You claim you flew across the ocean, parachuted into our town, risking rough men guarding the roads just to say you saw these two people sitting on a bench?"

"And swimming."

"Have you met this man before?" pointing at the defense attorney "Or this man?" pointing at the father of the defendant.

Jan replied in the negative, pointing at each and shaking his head. Luke interpreted, "No and No," pointing at each, also.

"I am having a hard time believing you could see all of this from your table rock."

Jan signaled his brother he would handle this. His struggle was not just with language.

Very slowly, in cadenced, precise English, he pronounced, "It was clear... like blood... on snow." Every word was crystal clear and very loud.

The defense attorney sat perfectly still. His client was at peace and fascinated.

The district attorney was not at peace. With more sarcasm, he mimicked Jan, "What does that mean, Blood... on...snow?"

Jan was livid and did not speak. Luke was furious but spoke in a clear, loud voice.

"Two years before, in winter, we, with our parents and little brother, were skiing in the Alps. Our mother carried our little brother. A hunter from the forest shot a crossbow bolt. It went through our mother and through our little brother. It was an accident, but the hunter threw away the crossbow and skied off a cliff and died, too. Our father carried our mother, and we together carried our little brother down to the mountain lodge. We washed the blood off them at our best. They were buried together, my brother in his Spiderman suit that he loved in our mother's arms." Luke could talk no more.

Thomas and Julia cried. He leaned against her and whispered, "Such courage."

Then Luke took a deep breath and continued softly, "That is why we do things. Our father said, 'Do not be afraid. Use your lives. Do great things.' That is why we came. "That is why we are not afraid of hard men. That is why we follow like shadows the special soldiers like our cousin who trains in our country. But we were very careful with the parachute." They had fulfilled their mission. They smiled peacefully at Nicolas.

The former alleged victim raised her hand. The judge acknowledged her, and she stood and spoke from where she was, "I said all along that nothing happened. I said the two boys from Harlem knew the truth. She would not believe me." Her mother sat beside her.

"Judge, I will move for a Dismissal."

"Denied." Everyone froze for a second. "I am entering a finding Not Guilty after one more piece of business. Step up here." He pointed at the district attorney, then at the defense attorney, then at the father of Nicolas. It was clearly not a request. He also asked Nicolas to join them.

"Your Honor, my client's father has nothing to do...."

"Bailiff, I am instructing you to escort the father and his attorney to my bench or to the jail for contempt. I see the sheriff at the back door of the courtroom, and he can act as a bailiff while you are gone." The judge finally sat and turned to the witnesses and told them, "I know you are tired, but I want you to remain standing so you can hear this." Looking at Luke and then at Jan, he said, I will be clear."

He signaled the court reporter closer to take down what he was going to say.

"You will not speak, or you will go to jail." He pointed slowly at the district attorney, at the defense attorney, and the father. "The young man on trial today deserves better than the three of you. Justice and innocence prevailed today, no thanks to you two or you either for that matter," this last with a glare at the district attorney.

"We cherish our system because of days like today. You two will personally guarantee the safety of these two witnesses even if they choose to go skydiving." He turned toward them and shook his head from side to side to cancel that suggestion. "I am driving out of town today, and I am giving you a direct order enforceable by contempt. If I see a single one of your myrmidons, I will put you both in jail. Now step back."

"The defendant will stand." The defendant stood in front of the table where his father and the defense attorney sat.

"I am finding you Not Guilty." Cheers and applause followed with the judge's approval. He raised his hand only to indicate he had more to say. "It is rare that a person has such loyal friends, especially since you have never actually met. I suggest that everyone meet outside the courtroom.

"Adjourned."

After consulting with the boys, the priest invited everyone to mass the next morning concelebrated with the bishop. High mass to be sung by the Brakhuis brothers.

Their father had arrived minutes before. He was very big. The father told his sons they would finish the school year in America, in this town, if possible, and return to the language camp next summer. Mr. Brakhuis indicated he might want to teach driver's education in America for a year or so.

Nicolas, with his mother beside him, spoke to the former victim's mother. He was most respectful. "I would like permission to visit you and your daughter at your house from time to time." Nicolas showed a small smile. I will attend school here this next semester and wanted to tell you myself."

"Thank you. Yes, thank you."

The next day after the mass, Julia said, "Robot, my father will arrive next week and has told me—no, has asked me to choose a high school in this vicinity. I choose your vicinity. Grandmother Nanette has indicated she could use a boarder. I could learn a lot from her."

"Someone should warn the school about all this...."

# RAM

John Rivas, medical doctor and psychiatrist, declared Ramiro brain dead at 3:47 p.m. on Saturday, September 12. Doctor T. Bach, his assistant, concurred three minutes later. Normally, this would have been sad, not an admission of their defeat by a strange child.

These grave pronouncements were made despite the fact that Ramiro was clearly visible outside the giant picture window of Cottage Two, helping the men irrigate the cotton fields that surrounded the Center. He was using a long-handled shovel, closing off a row that had been irrigated sufficiently and removing a few shovelfuls of the heavy clay soil to allow the next furrow to receive water. Meanwhile, Ramiro's new public-school classmates were enjoying their first-weekend freedom after a grueling two-day week of the new school year.

He felt his first two classes ever had gone rather well the day before. He was wearing his best and only shirt, gauze thin and white, his best and only pants, khaki, and his beaten but polished black shoes with socks. He thought the socks were a nice touch. Except for the new socks, they were the same clothes he had worn, picking onions and cotton all summer in the Lower Rio Grande valley until he himself was picked from a farm workers' camp near Brownsville and sent to a home for emotionally disturbed children for possible admission. Meanwhile, at school, there came a roll call with P.E. Coach Maguire ("Cracker" to the faculty). All was normal until he called Ramiro's name. Ram, as he was called, was embarrassed to have his name called out, so his response to the huge psychopathic Cracker was clear.

"Your mother."

Every child in the class froze. Instinctively they knew that Ram's answer was not a good idea. The Neanderthal smiled and asked to speak to Ram in the hall and took his board with him. The swat sounded like the crack of a bat. The coach showed more promise as a disciplinarian than as, well, than as anything else. He started the roll call over, not at Ram's name, but at the beginning…

Ramiro gave the same answer to his name being called the second time.

Second verse, same as the first except Swat, Swat.

Every teacher learns to establish discipline early, if it is going to be established at all. From that point of view, Ram was a god sent. This fourth-grade class was forever converted—roll call, third time…from the start.

Ram's name was called, and he was hyperventilating and very vigilant but silent. The coach called his name again.

"Ramiro."

"President."

"Not 'president,' 'present.' Just say 'Here."

"Here, coach."

For some reason, Ramiro associated violence with coaching: there are small gaps in everyone's education. Also, Ram had never heard the word "present" even at Christmas. But here was a guy Ram could understand. Blunt. Clear. Direct. Helpful. Not like Doctor Rivas.

Ram knew that the tests set for the next day, Saturday, were to prove he was not very bright and did not belong at the Center. His view of the doctor's plan was essentially correct.

The contest was scheduled for three-thirty at the famous table of Cottage Two. The boys had built this sturdy cable-spool-based table with the help of Super Two, their head counselor. They had the hardest code of all the cottages and, with supervision, governed themselves from this table. They felt they had a say in who was ready to leave and who should be admitted. They actually did, thanks to the brilliance and tolerance of the prior cottage supervisor who instituted positive peer pressure and the brilliance of the Center's administrator, Jean Patrice.

Dr. Rivas's instructions to Ram the next afternoon seemed clear. "Ramiro, you and I are going to do word association. When I say a word, you say the first word that comes into your mind. Do you completely understand my instructions?"

Suspicion and glaring from the huge brown eyes. "Yes."

"Chair."

"Chair."

"Mother."

"Mother."

"Door."

"Door."

"This is not working, Ramiro. You are just saying the word I said."

"When you say a word, that's what I think."

The group had insisted on attending and watched, silent but fascinated.

"I think you are resisting, Ramiro. Let's try it another way. I want you to say any other word except the word I say. The first word is 'Mother.'"

Remembering yesterday, "Will I get in trouble?"

"No, of course not. Mother."

"Madre."

"Door."

"Puerta."

Ramiro had agreed that the boys of Cottage Two, known as The Group, should be present for these tests since, if accepted, he would live with them. Doctor Rivas more or less appealed to them to see that Ram was even too limited to take the tests. "This isn't working either. You are just saying the same word in Spanish."

"A pigeon is not smart, but it lands on a telephone wire. An ant can build everything again after rain. I am doing what you say." The Group thought this was at least as bright as anything the doctor had said. The doctor's assistant spoke.

"Doctor, maybe I can help. Ramiro, I am Doctor Bach. I am your friend. I am going to ask you questions, and all you have to do is answer, ok?"

More glares and more suspicion. "Ok."

"What's your mom like?"

"Fish."

"No."

"She does, too. She likes fish. You don't even know my mother."

The group and now even the staff thought that was great. Ram began to cry but would not touch his face. Huge tears from huge brown eyes rolled down his face and dripped onto his tissue-thin white shirt, the only one he owned. He had washed it in a basin the night before, using hand soap. His calloused hands rested on the thighs of his khaki pants.

Ramiro was sure they were cheating and that they were saying he was too stupid to live here. The food was good, and the children were less abusive than his family, and he had been allowed to work as hard as a man with the men who tended the fields surrounding the Center.

The good doctor took over the interview again from his assistant. "Ramiro, this is your last chance to stay here at the center with your friends." The doctor glared briefly at the audience around the table. The doctor had the sense to know the Group's loyalty was now with Ramiro. "We need to put some closure to this. If you can use the word 'closure,' I will agree for you to stay."

The Group glanced at each other and thought that stunk. The odds of any child in the fourth grade knowing that word were slim. The odds of an emotionally disturbed child removed from an abusive farmworker family with very limited English knowing the word "closure" were even thinner.

He had heard that word at this giant table where they all now sat. The mean counsel had said it to him just this morning at breakfast. Not helpful like the coach, just mean.

With the timing and skill of a true champ, Ram delivered his punch. "Close your mouth, or the flies will get out."

That was just before the psychologist and psychiatrist declared him brain dead and sent him outside to work, but the real vote was in.

The doctors thought it was a punishment to send him outside to help the men irrigate the cotton fields. Ram thought it was an admission that they had cheated and that he was being rewarded. The administrator, a very courageous woman, finally allowed the Group's vote to stand.

———•———

The members of the Group were trained how to answer the house phone. It should have been, "Cottage Two, Larry speaking," "Cottage Two, David speaking."

Doctor Rivas called the cottage two weeks after Ram was admitted, and Ram answered, "What?"

"Who is this?"

Ram recognized the doctor's voice and suspected a continuation of the doctor's attempts to disparage his intelligence and said, "You can't fool me, you're Doctor Rivas," and hung up the phone. The doctor would visit the cottage after that but would not use the phone.

Ram lived at the Center for two years. During that time, his idioms were slowly adopted. "I have to see the doctor about two of my feet." When talking on the phone, "Let me switch to another ear." When he aged out, he went to live in another city at a center for teens preparing for independent living. He moved to Mexico for a while and became a deputy sheriff in a small northern border town. When the sheriff died of a heart attack, Ram took over briefly and worked even more briefly with another former member of the Group. He was so successful, they both had to leave town quickly.

# THE BIG TRUCK

It is Monday in the break room of the district attorney's office. The trial team supervisor is asking his newest misdemeanor attorney what is on her docket. He is screaming and rude which does not bother him but which does explain why he must repeat the office's sensitivity training class. He is being fairly careful for him.

Law for the hard of hearing, as those he supervises called it.

"You've never actually practiced civil law, like what an attractive nuisance is, right?"

That witty remark typically means something like a swimming pool without a fence near a grade school. She knows the remark regarding her is pretty accurate, so she ignores it and outlines her morning. "I have plea hearings all morning. Five cases have attorneys; they will plead or have some lame reason for a continuance."

"So, Clarence Darrow, attorney number three, knows how prepared you are and announces ready. Are you ready to represent this great state and prosecute that case this morning? By the way, have the five attorneys presented motions for continuances?"

"I'm not sure, but they are never prepared."

"One of your cases was public intoxication which you raised to DWI. Why? Why are you smarter than the police officer who charged public intoxication? Who is the defense attorney?" This barrage is typical. His misdemeanor attorneys call this level of supervision Defcon One.

"Noah Joseph, but I heard he's really over the hill."

"Are your officers upstairs? Did the older one sign the arrest affidavit or the younger one? How did you get this case? Public intoxication cases are not even filed with us."

"I was assigned to the justice of the peace courts for the week and saw it filed there. I filed it as a higher offense and screened it myself instead of sending it to our screening section."

"Did the officers perform any tests on this guy?" Field sobriety? Breath test?"

"The Supreme Court says the officers can arrest him for any Class C violation except speeding and possession of an open container. *Atwater v. City of Lago Vista.*

"You did not answer my question. You answered whether they could arrest without a warrant. You should run for president. Very good, grasshopper. I will be in the courtroom, and I want to see you prove or offer to prove that the defendant was driving drunk."

"He wasn't driving. He was 'operating a motor vehicle.'"

"This gets better and better. Did you attend my last CLE on DWI and public intoxication? Is the inside of a car always a public place? Continuing Legal Education means continuing, and it assumes you know something to start with."

At 9:00, the bailiff announced, "County Court at Law Number Two is now in session, "Honorable Margaret Ash presiding. Be seated."

Cynics, including the supervisor in the back of the courtroom, wondered how she ever became a judge. She was polite, prepared, punctual, and fair.

There had been a commotion in the courtroom minutes earlier. Attorney Noah Joseph, the last of the great circus attorneys of his generation, was seated at the defense table, silent and apparently comatose. He was normally in complete control of his case, renowned for his research preparation, for his knowledge of the law, for his flamboyance. His physician was sitting to his left.

Judge Ash nodded toward the physician and asked him, "Could you identify yourself and explain what is happening here?"

Instead of the physician, the assistant district attorney stood and said to the court, "Your Honor, this entire charade is simply a crude attempt to obtain a continuance in a case where Mr. Joseph is not prepared. His theatrics are well known throughout the building."

"Thank you, Assistant District Attorney. Now we will hear from the person I asked to speak." That was legalese for "Smack." She nodded at the man seated on one side of Attorney Noah Joseph.

Standing and constantly watching the listless attorney seated beside him, the doctor addressed the court,

"Judge, I am Doctor Armando Rueda. I was called here twenty minutes ago by E.M.S. attendants. They are waiting just outside the courtroom to transport Mr. Joseph. My patient may have experienced a vascular incident of some sort, possibly a stroke. Or, he may be disoriented due to a depletion of potassium, salt, or electrolytes. He has been administered a strong dose of aspirin with Gatorade by the defendant to counter those possibilities." He stopped talking and looked at the defendant, and pondered the medical ramifications of such action. "Blood has been drawn and is already on its way to the hospital lab to ascertain the cause of this uncharacteristic condition. He is still here because I do not know if he can absorb anything happening right now, but I can tell the court he has been my client for twenty years, and I know him. It is in his medical best interest to know if it is possible for him to know that this incident does not harm his client."

The man sitting to the right of the attorney raised his hand.

The judge acknowledged him, and so he stood and spoke. "Your Honor, I am just the defendant, but this can be resolved in less than five minutes if you would allow me. Then my attorney can go in peace."

"Any objection, State?"

"Yes, your honor. I vigorously object."

"No, your honor," from the back of the courtroom.

"Ah, the chief of the misdemeanor trial courts. The State has spoken. Proceed, defendant."

"Judge, my attorney has instructed me regarding what to do in case he gets hit by a big truck. That's sort of what's happened here. I can follow his exact instructions and finish this. I will represent myself with the written help of Mr. Joseph." He patted a legal-sized folder before him, identical to the one before his attorney.

The judge said nothing but nodded. The trial chief nodded, also.

"I am asking the older patrol officer to simply stand where he is and answer if the motor of my car was running?"

A bristling young man almost jumped out of his chair and said, jabbing in the defendant's direction, "It was running, and that means this guy was operating a motor vehicle and can be charged with driving while intoxicated."

"Your honor, my attorney's big truck instructions say that if the younger patrol officer jumps up and answers, I am to ask for the older patrol officer."

"Your honor, I sincerely doubt that any instructions say that. I would like to see them."

"Judge, the front of my big truck folder says ATTORNEY-CLIENT PRIVILEGE… Judge, tick tock, tick tock."

The judge looked around the court, "Is the other patrol officer present?"

"Yes, I am here, your honor."

"Repeat the question, defendant."

"My car was parked off the shoulder of the road, and I was asleep, right?"

"Yes, I had to open the car door and shake you to see if you were awake or even alive."

"Are you familiar with this model car?"

"Yes, I have one like it."

"Was the car running or not?"

"No, on this model car, the doors will remain locked unless the car is parked and the motor is turned off. I could not have opened the door if the motor was on. That is why you were only charged with public intoxication. You cannot be charged with operating a motor vehicle unless the motor is turned on."

"Was this explanation in your arrest affidavit or sworn complaint?"

"Yes, of course."

"Does the video from your body camera show what you just said?"

"Yes, and it was filed with the case."

"Is the State moving to dismiss?"

"Yes, your honor, but the state intends to refile the public intoxication complaint."

From the back of the courtroom, "The state moves to dismiss and not refile, your honor."

"The Master has spoken. Defendant, your case is hereby dismissed. Please help the doctor escort your amazing attorney to the attendants outside. Oh, Miss State, young patrol officer, may I see you both at the bench?" More legalese for "This is not a request."

The young officer was walking away and said, "I need to be in another court." "Bailiff, the officer needs an escort."

At the academy, every officer is taught to take command of every situation—almost every situation. It requires perspective to accept that a person in a black robe without any weapons or physical strength represents an entire branch of government and is— in this room—in command.

The officer did a U-turn and approached the bench.

"First. Miss State. *Brady v. Maryland,* United States Supreme Court, requires that you turn over everything that tends to exonerate the defendant. Otherwise, you lose the case. Maybe nothing happens to you.

The Michael Morton Act in this State goes much further. If you distort or fail to disclose evidence to the defendant, you should have known about or even could have known about, as in this case, you are subject to losing your license after losing the case. I want a report on this bench by the end of your workday outlining those two pieces of law and explaining why I should not report this violation to the State Bar's Grievance Committee. Since I see no justification for your not knowing and applying these two landmark cases, your response may include a plea to the mercy of the court. If the courtroom is locked, slide your response under the door.

"Now, officer, I would prefer that you never testify in my court again. If you do, I will want your superior present. The defendant's car was impounded, he had to pay fees to get it out. That was fair. He lost a day's wages for today's unnecessary hearing; that was not fair. I would like to know he was compensated for today's wages by one day after your next paycheck. If you decline my suggestion, I will have a suggestion for your superior and internal affairs regarding perjury charges. Before you tell me that you were not sworn in, I will remind you that you are an officer of this court and always under a duty to tell the truth, sworn in or not. Adjourned."

---

"So, grasshopper, I am happy to announce that Attorney Joseph has made an almost complete recovery and could resume his practice as early as next week. He may even be well enough to file a Michael Morton grievance against you himself. I see that you skipped lunch and have prepared motions to sanction the judge and the defendant for practicing law and medicine without the proper licenses. I see your afternoon docket is full, but if you choose to obey the court's order, you will find my brilliant lectures on what constitutes a public place, on operating a motor vehicle, and on the Michael Morton Act on your computer on our common drive. My next legal education topic will be defenses against jailable contempt, but it is not ready yet. For now, I will give you the short version—there aren't any.

There is lunch at the reception desk for you. I will take your court this afternoon so you can respond to the court's instructions. In exchange for giving you my lunch and my afternoon, I will expect you to help me present the next legal seminar, assuming you are not disbarred by then and not fired for filing a grievance against the judge.

"Later, you could do a search to see if this morning's defendant has a law license or medical license or both. He sounded pretty smart. Now he has courtroom experience and no criminal record.

"One last thing. Find out what our primary duty is. I will give you a hint. It is part of the oath you took when you were sworn in as an assistant district attorney. It's in the Code of Criminal Procedure toward the very front. Something about every prosecutor's primary duty is not to convict but to see that justice is done."

# THE ALLIANCE

She fully expected to have her probation revoked and to be sent to jail. She was seventeen and had just admitted to the assistant principal that she had retaliated on her computer for a threat she had received.

Allison knew that since her response to the threat was both vague and conditional, she could not be charged with a new crime. Her advertisement for a ditch digger implied she needed a place to put her nemesis, the snitch. She also knew that it could be enough for her probation officer to try to revoke her. She knew that before she sent her email.

She had been left in the office to think about her crime, but Allison's moral compass did not work well yet. Her view was if there was enough evidence, she was guilty. Otherwise, she must not have done anything wrong.

The assistant principal had called Allison's mother at work. "You need to come to the school immediately in regard to your daughter."

"Is she injured?"

"No, she threatened another student, and your presence is required immediately."

"I have to keep this job to put food on the table and to pay the rent. You are a grown man. Handle it yourself." No Tsunami mommy, no drama mama, no smother mother.

His day was not going to get better with the next phone call. "This is Detective Eliot. May I help you?"

"Yes, sir. This is the assistant principal at your daughter's school. As the parent of the victim, you might want some input regarding the punishment for the student who threatened her."

"Thanks for calling, but I am really busy. I am a cybercrime detective with an enormous workload. I saw what my daughter wrote to the other girl.

My daughter is not a victim. Handle it yourself, but if my daughter is not punished, I will make time for an appointment with the principal. Goodbye."

He thought about calling Allison's probation officer but did not want to be insulted a third time in ten minutes.

"I'm not calling your probation officer. I'm handling this myself."

She could see through that and almost see her mother's footprints on this guy but acted appreciative.

"You and Marcia are going to be offered the same deal. Thirty hours of community service, fifteen if you perform them together."

Because her criminal case was deferred and could ultimately be dismissed, she was allowed to work in a sensitive area, a trauma/ rehabilitation center.

The advice was plentiful. Marcia had received advice from her alleged friends concerning Allison. Basically, the advice was, "She is low-brow, blue-collar. Demolish her with further internet taunts and insults." Allison's advice, on the other hand, came from her kickboxing instructor. Marcia's father and Allison's mother had remarkably similar advice, work together and get this done.

The two young ladies met in front of the trauma center as arranged by their parents. Just the sight of each other almost undid that plan. The idiotic threats she had sent on her computer were nothing compared to what Marcia's detective father had guaranteed if she failed to complete this community service. Allison's mother said, "I cannot afford time away from work, and we cannot afford a fine. Handle this."

"For the fifteen hours we have to work together, the people inside will think we are best friends."

"Agreed." Allison was thinking, *"Ice queen,"* but extended her hand and said, "Truce. For the next two weeks, no one will come between us."

Marcia half expected to be thrown across the parking lot with some wrestling move but extended her manicured hand anyway. *"At least she didn't spit in her hand first."*

Both were as good as their word. Marcia introduced herself at the front desk and then said, "This is my friend, Allison. Arrangements have been made that we will work together." Allison could take a punch or a kick, but that part about being Marcia's friend nearly staggered her. She figured her part was to keep a straight face and keep her mouth shut, which she did manage.

From 6:00 to 7:30 every evening for two weeks, they were assigned to read to patients, bring them water, escort those with walkers or in wheelchairs from the dining hall to their rooms. They were not to move them from chair to bed, and they were not to do any of the jobs assigned to the nurses or nursing assistants.

They ended their first tour of duty in the room of a man who was recovering from a head injury from an automobile accident. He could not walk or speak yet but appeared to be typing at a small table on a tablet. He was already in his pajamas when the nursing assistant came in to put him to bed. She put him into the bed and then picked up his tablet. The man was very agitated by that and reached weakly for it. She first pushed the button for the main menu and then pushed the button for do not save. Curious. Very curious.

The nursing assistant shut the tablet and straightened up a few things. Despite the man's agony and the surprise on the "volunteers" faces, she began her patronizing patter. "We need to begin each day fresh, Mr. Anderson. Writing stories to your son will not bring him back. We must all face facts. You are getting stronger each day and need to concentrate on your improvement. No clutter from the past."

Leaving only his night light on, she escorted Marcia and Allison into the hallway. It had subdued lighting, beautiful carpet, wooden handicap rails on both sides, and beautiful pictures donated over the years by residents or their families in appreciation of the care they had received. Both girls suspected that Mr. Anderson would not be among future donors.

"Mr. Anderson's son is still alive, but only barely. He is in a coma as a result of the same accident. He is writing him the same old stories he used to tell him. The family said the son had even numbered the stories. I guess probably because he disliked them so much."

They met briefly in the same parking lot after signing out. They were not the same two who had entered earlier. Allison's moral machinery within a few minutes of witnessing actual evil was suddenly operating properly. Any slights she had received from Marcia were fading fast by comparison. Marcia's epiphany was equally sudden and consequential. For the first time she could remember she was outraged by a genuine injustice.

"How do you want to handle this?"

"Could your father show you how to retrieve what was erased on the tablet?"

"He would need the tablet. It might have to be 'Bring Your Dad to Work Night.' I will arrange it. Can you locate the son?"

"Yes. I will locate him. Maybe your father could get the accident report. There is so much to do we might have to quit school—joke alert. I will work on the nursing assistant. She needs to be handled with care. I'll bet she's immune to sodium pentothal and will change her story. I will be very careful."

The next day at school, the instigators were eager to cause damage between the two. The internet was humming with purported quotes from Marcia wishing Allison death or evil. All went unanswered. This snub angered the instigators, who escalated insults against both girls. "Who's your new chimpanion?" This was sent to Marcia and then to Allison. "I am not her chimpanion. I am her companzee."

Marcia received a message at noon saying, "He is in the same center two stories below his father. He is in an induced coma to give his brain time to heal. He is not about to die." It was signed, "your friend, Allison."

Two weeks had passed, but Marcia and Allison continued to meet at the rehab center.

In the room of Mr. Anderson were the center's administrator, Detective Eliot, and the nursing assistant.

"Mr. Anderson, I am Patrick Eliot. Some young ladies told me your stories mean a great deal to you. I have retrieved them from your computer," with a quick look at the nurse's assistant, "and I have had them transcribed and read out loud. The reader is a patient here. He has some memory problems and is weak, but is making improvement."

The administrator took it from there. "The patient, your son, is too weak to visit you for now, but he will. For now, he wants you to hear one of your own stories.

The voice on the recording was weak but dramatic and humorous. "Oh, Pop. Not story fifty-six again." It began, "When I was a boy, the man who cut the grass with his sons had an old black truck with a crank in the front that had to be used to start the truck. Later, the trucks got starters...."

Mr. Anderson sat in wonderment in the very pleasant company of Detective Eliot.

The administrator meanwhile excused herself and signaled for the nurse's assistant to follow.

In the hallway, she said, "My first inclination was to fire you immediately. Two young ladies stepped forward and said, if I choose not to do that, they would handle this themselves and supervise your community service for fifteen hours. They want you to help them bring Mr. Anderson's son to visit him each evening. I will allow that. You will work with them as a volunteer during those fifteen hours. If you are not inclined, you will be terminated. I will review your employment at the end of that time."

# SANTIAGO LANDEROS

Oscar and Lupe, the cook and gardener, with Noe, their ten-year-old grandson, were cleaning the living room of the family house as if they were moving in, not out. Being older, they were informally in charge wherever they went when the family was not there. They were raising Noe, who was family. Several people here and at the family ranch in Mexico were considered family who were not related. Everyone was considered family. Alicia was the teenaged daughter of the chauffeur, and she assisted Oscar and Lupe. Alicia's father, Don Victor, still called the chauffeur, was recovering these last six months at the ranch in Durango from multiple bullet wounds. He and his daughter and everyone at the ranch—family.

The young man about to address this part of his family was Santiago, Santiago Landeros, the very young owner of this house and owner of the entire ranch in Mexico where they were all headed. Santiago's mother and father had crossed into Juarez to shop at the open market on the 16th of September Avenue. A gang of thugs had put down boards and large branches across the road to stop the sedan Don Victor was driving. He had pulled up to the barricade and asked the group of men to move the boards and branches.

Instead, they demanded? "Que barrio?" What neighborhood? Don Victor knew these words meant nothing but violence would follow. He attempted to drive over the barricade and was met with a hail of gunfire which killed both parents and severely wounded him. Unable even to attend the double funeral held in the small mission church, Don Victor had been taken to the family ranch leaving his daughter Alicia at the house in El Paso. Alicia was only twelve and had become a ward of the family but was helpful to Oscar and Lupe, who were getting older.

The young man standing before the collection of servants and wards was one of the last two survivors of his family and the sole heir of this house and the ranch in Durango under Mexican law.

His half-brother, Diego, was his only sibling, his closest relative. He was twenty-five and was very angry even at the funerals. At the cemetery after the burial, he told Santiago, "I can run the ranch. I am a man. I will not take orders from someone who has never shaved. It is not fair that because my mother was not married to our father, I should not own part of the ranch."

"We will solve this when I come to the ranch."

Santiago reflected on this conversation. What Diego said was true. He was an excellent rancher and farmer. He watched out for the workers. He grew corn on the most fertile land and relied on God's blessing and His rain. Now that the nearby town had built a dam for its own survival from flooding, the vast ranch had a guaranteed market for its cheese, beef, and corn. Only this one subject caused Diego to brood and listen to bad advice from lawyers in Parral who were trying to persuade him that he could take the ranch from Santiago for a certain amount they would receive. Santiago was only five years older than Alicia, but he spoke with authority and gravity as if he were the very young king of a vast empire. In a way, he was.

The talk was fairly brief. Everyone knew what would be said. "I will be gone for two days. I go to put flowers on the grave of my mother and father from all of us. I expect to return tomorrow night or at the latest the morning after that and go with you all to the ranch. As always, Oscar will make any necessary decisions in my absence. There is enough food and no money. If necessary, Oscar has a bank draft that will get you all back to the ranch. I expect to go with you, but if you return to the ranch without me and are not satisfied with what is happening there, you will take note of what is wrong. Take no action. The family appreciates your continued service, and your compensation will be on time at the end of next month as usual as soon as the sale of this house is complete."

He was dressed like a very poor king. He was wearing *huaraches*, leather sandals with soles made from used tires. The advantage was that they lasted a very long time. A baseball cap, summer shorts, and a faded blue t-shirt completed his royal ensemble. He carried no identification. He had a passport he could use for identification but would not carry it since he would stay in El Paso. His knapsack held only a bottle of water. He would not allow Lupe to deplete the food in the house. His dignity prohibited her from crying in front of him.

To Oscar alone, he said, "If you go to the ranch and my half-brother is there, please tell him I will meet with him as soon as I arrive. No matter what he says, I will deal with it. He is very angry at the moment. Protect yourself and the family from him, but otherwise, do not harm him. He is a good man, and we will have peace at the ranch. Please send my regards to Don Victor." Then to Alicia and Noe, he said, "Obey Oscar and Lupe." Then with mock gravity, "The master has spoken."

As he left the house of so many good memories, he remembered his father's stories of how he could hear the morning bugle call from the Pershing gate of Fort Bliss. The father told him that in the afternoon from this house, he could hear shooting from the firing range of the police academy along Scenic Drive, which wound around the eastern side of the Franklin Mountains.

His parents had made arrangements for the sale of the house in their wills. The house was being sold furnished minus his furniture. The buyers would take possession within weeks. The proceeds would fund his college and law school if all went well. Thanks to his early college classes in high school, he would start college in one year and one month as a junior. As a condition of the sale, he would live in the garage apartment while finishing high school. The petition for his emancipation had been ready for filing at the district court since his sixteenth birthday, that would allow him to enter legally binding contracts in the United States, but so far, his parents' foresight had taken care of everything.

After half an hour of walking, he came to the edge of a long, lush valley in the middle of the desert city where he would spend the night. He crossed over the steep hill with creosote and cactus topped by railroad tracks which formed one side of the valley. The low stables and adjoining corral could hold twenty horses. There were officers' polo ponies for the nearby Armstrong playing field at the edge of the Fort Bliss main gate, and there were horses of individual families who could not otherwise keep horses in the city. Santiago's father had bought a very small horse from the stable's owner, and it now lived at the ranch and represented the ranch in local races.

The horses were comfortable with him, and the stable owner always welcomed him. He walked each horse in the exercise area, which extended the length of this valley several blocks long. Then he brushed each and made sure there was water and fresh straw in each stall. Two of the owner's sons came later when it was evening and greeted Santiago. They were happy to see him for several reasons. They liked him, and he had already done their work.

They would stay for a while but would not have to spend the night because Santiago was most reliable.

They played songs on an old guitar they kept in the tack room and talked about their futures, but eventually, they decided to get home. In his father's day at ten o'clock, all the light signals in the entire city began flashing red. For the cars, it meant to stop, then proceed with caution. For the juveniles, it meant they were already violating the curfew. They gave Santiago the snacks they had brought for tomorrow morning and bid him goodnight. He chose two saddle blankets for the night, one for cover and one for a pillow. It rained lightly during the night. The breeze almost always came from the southwest carrying the fragrance of the desert creosote bushes into the city and the stable. There was no lightning or thunder. The rain hitting on the galvanized roof was pleasant and had a tranquilizing effect on the horses. The sky was overcast, and sounds were muffled.

The next morning before dawn, he checked every horse's water, put a few carrots and a few apples in his knapsack, and left for the municipal rose garden nearby. Dawn was breaking when he arrived to see workers with a faded primer grey pickup pulling a long trailer filled with bleating goats just arriving.

He formally introduced himself to Miguel and Simon, who had cleverly entered a contract with the city to keep the numerous rosebushes of what looked like a garden amphitheater trimmed. Santiago spoke to them with great respect. They were comfortable with his business proposal. He requested six roses in exchange for unloading and supervising the goats until noon, when he would help reload them back into the trailer. He smelled faintly of horses and hay, and the goats followed him willingly.

The goats were distributed on each of the tiers of the garden. They ate the extra foliage off the bushes and ate the grass between the bushes, which would cause the bushes to produce more roses. By noon they had done their job. The men thought Santiago would have a really hard time getting the goats into the trailer. He sacrificed one of the carrots from the stable to lure the leader back into the trailer. The others followed. Miguel was very impressed and made a mental note to bring a few carrots from his farm in Ysleta on each visit to the municipal rose garden.

With his roses in his knapsack, the stems wrapped in damp newspaper, Santiago backtracked past the stables, over the railroad tracks, down Wilson

Way to Happer Street on his walk to the cemetery called Evergreen. He wanted to stop first at the chapel of San Juan and leave two roses at the altar.

He did not expect any problems since he was passing through middle-income neighborhoods with well-trimmed yards. People who were outdoors, despite the heat, would wave or say hello.

Santiago was blessed with being bilingual. The city in his father's day was mostly Anglo and mostly friendly. As he got closer to the San Juan area, he saw two boys about his age appearing to block his path. He saw trouble coming. He spoke most respectfully to them.

"Hola, Caballeros." (Hello, gentlemen). The most formal way to greet other young men.

The boys wanted to intimidate him and said, "Que barrio?" (What neighborhood?)

It was the question gangsters had asked his parents before they were killed.

There was no good answer for these two headed down a criminal path.

"No barrio, Señores." Now he spoke to them in English. "My parents were murdered, their house will be sold, and I am without family or house or barrio. I am going to the cemetery to pay them respect."

The larger of the two boys said, "You must pay respect to our gang, too. You cannot cross through our neighborhood unless you pay us our quota."

Proving that he was going to become a lawyer, Santiago addressed him. "Sir, I have an apple and a carrot, my wages from yesterday, and six roses for my parents' grave. I have nothing else but what little I wear. I will gladly give you two roses for your quota to honor your mothers."

He took two roses from the knapsack and offered them to the larger boy.

The larger boy took one of the roses by the flower and whipped the stem backhanded down and across Santiago's face. A thorn caught just above Santiago's right cheekbone and cut a furrow all the way to his chin. Tiny drops of blood dripped down onto Santiago's faded blue t-shirt.

"That was for your mother."

Time stood still. He could see his mother clearly and hear her talking to him, repeating the beautiful advice she had given him as a small child. "If someone calls me names or insults me to upset you, be at peace. That will be a gift to me. I love you." The witness expected Santiago to try to kill his assailant. So did the assailant. A killing today would cloud his future and dishonor his mother. His decision was written on his face — a radiant smile.

"In honor of both our mothers, we will be friends for life. We will be family. I cannot fight family." He wiped some of the blood from his face with the palm of his right hand and extended it to both his new family members, his new friends. "Amigos, my name is Santiago Landeros."

The stunned witness said to the assailant, "Shake his hand and tell him our names."

Afterward, Santiago gave them each another rose for their mothers and still had two for the cemetery.

That night Lupe cried at the sight of Santiago's face. Wisely, she dabbed the cut with hydrogen peroxide. Oscar said, "It will be shallow, but a very handsome scar. It will define you." Lupe raised her eyes to heaven for help and responded, "Hombres."

Oscar and Lupe had moved the furniture Santiago would use for the remainder of his high school to his garage apartment and made sure his small kitchen was equipped. Then they packed for their final trip to the ranch.

The next morning was busy. Lupe made delicious huevos rancheros for breakfast, eggs on corn tortillas with a sauce of tomatoes, cheese, and chopped chile. Then everyone made the house perfect for the buyers. An old friend of his parents arrived at eleven in a very big Suburban to take Oscar and Lupe and their grandson Noe and Alicia, the daughter of the wounded chauffeur, and Santiago to the huge Juarez bus terminal, which served all of northernmost Mexico.

They traveled from Juarez through Chihuahua to Parral, arriving early the next morning after a night of fitful sleep on the bus. One of the regulations of Mexico is that a bus must stop at any railroad track crossing the highway and turn off its lights.

Lupe had packed a meal of different burritos, some of the chile rellenos, some beans with cheese, and some chile verde. They bought coffee and orange and pineapple flavored sodas from the street vendors. In a plaza near the town's main church, Lupe spread a blanket where they ate.

Santiago had two errands which took him one hour. He had a thin envelope and a packet of papers in a thick business envelope which was sealed when he returned. The thin envelope contained a copy of a letter from his brother's attorneys promising to pay the bill for preparation of the thick packet he carried. He did not mention what he had told them for trying to steal the ranch but indicated they would not be coming to the ranch any time soon. He did not speak of the thick envelope from his family's regular attorney.

From there, they boarded a train to the mining town of Santa Barbara. Very young soldiers guarded the train with very big automatic weapons. Beer was sold on the train. The train rocked along through the last of the Chihuahua desert landscape of ocotillo and creosote and sage and cactus and large prairie grass areas.

Santiago's beautiful cousin, Chela, greeted them at the train station and insisted they all stay at her house for the night. Otherwise, they would arrive in Rosario, the town nearest the ranch, in the nighttime and still have to drive to the ranch on what was not really a road. Chela was a teacher of English and Spanish and had the summer off. Her husband was a pilot but was on a short vacation, also.

Their house was adobe stuccoed white and very cool even in the heat. There was an open courtyard at the center of the house with a small fountain. The top half of each long bedroom window opened so each room could receive a cross breeze in the night and still have privacy provided by the heavy curtains across the lower three-fourths of the windows. Beto, Chela's husband, remembered everyone from their wedding and said, "Chela's family was so generous to us at our wedding we want you to enjoy a meal I am preparing." They ate tacos al carbon with cilantro and guacamole and chopped tomatoes and lettuce.

The next morning it was back to the train. The train would travel backward to Rosario, the end of the line. It went backward on the way so it could come back through Santa Barbara without having to turn around.

There were more relatives in Rosario. Aunt Isela ran a small store and took care of her father, Tio Paulo. Santiago had two cousins whom everyone thought of as twins. The townspeople affectionately called them "the chattering squirrels." The ranch truck had been left in town for Santiago's use, and by noon, after a traditional meal of tomato-based Fideo soup with shredded chicken and cilantro and slices of avocado, they left for the ranch.

Diego, Santiago's brother by another mother, was out inspecting the corn crop, which was important to the ranch's economy. He was expecting the travelers today and was also avoiding them. He knew he had to come to a resolution about the ranch and dreaded it.

He saw Santiago approaching on the ranch racehorse as it was called. His father had selected it from the stables where Santiago had recently spent the night. It was not big but had a great heart. Diego thought, "Like its rider."

Any harsh words Diego might have for his brother melted when Santiago removed his cowboy hat and Diego saw the red streak on his face. In a murderous tone, he said, "Who did that to you?"

"Shaving accident. Hola, Diego. I heard you are getting married. I bring you a wedding present," handing him the papers that had been prepared at the family attorney's office in Parral. "It is the deed to the ranch, exactly as father instructed."

"I don't understand. I thought we were going to fight."

"I guess we could. But no. You take the ranch. I'll take the United States."

They were off their horses now—a great *embrazo*. Diego held him by the shoulders but pushed him away a little so that he could see his face. Through his tears, he said, "But your looks, that's all you had." Both were laughing and crying now.

"What will you do?"

"I will be an attorney in under seven years, and then I will marry and have a career."

------•——•——•------

And so it was that in seven years and four months, Santiago was sworn in as an attorney and hired at a small district attorney's office in a small town in West Texas. For some reason, much of the center of the state is called West Texas. His first day on the job was his last, which created a future he could not have dreamed of.

There was nothing else happening in the entire criminal district for his first day, so the D.A. assigned him to a justice of the peace court where the judge was not required to be an attorney but was expected to follow the rules of judicial conduct as taught in the annual seminars that every judge was required to attend. A few attendants taught themselves what they wanted to hear in the hallways and lounges and ignored the presenters when they disagreed.

Santiago was starting to introduce himself when the judge spotted the defendant.

"The school called me about you. They say you disrespected a teacher and that you think you are a regular terror."

Santiago looked around to see if the judge had an office. Some judges called their offices "their chambers." Not being sure, Santiago asked the judge, "May I speak to you in private?"

"Whatever you have to say can be said in front of these fine folks. Most of them are from the school."

"With total respect, your honor, it is against the code of judicial conduct to allow anyone to contact you and discuss the facts of the case. This student, a freshman, has the right to a fair and impartial hearing before a neutral magistrate."

"You seem confused as to which side you are on. This is the school district, son. We like to support our school. These are their employees. You are defending the defendant."

"This morning, I took an oath as a prosecutor and swore that my primary duty would be to seek justice. In an effort to do that, I would like the court to call the case and allow me to call my first witness."

"All right. I am calling the case of the State of Texas versus Pedro Gutierrez, who is charged with abusive language toward a teacher in a public place, to wit, a public high school.

"How do you plead?"

"Not guilty."

"Son, I'm expecting you to call an employee of the school district."

"The State calls an employee of the school district, Mary Fresquez.

"Were you employed by the school district on the date of this event between this student and a teacher at the high school?"

"Yes, sir. The teacher told the student in Spanish to get out of the building, and the student told the teacher he was not his teacher and also that he could not talk to him that way."

"When the teacher told the student to leave the building after school, did he tell him. *'Vayase'* that is to say, 'Leave the building'?"

"No, sir."

"Did he tell him, *'Quitate'* like 'Get out of here.'"

"No, sir. The teacher told him, "*Largate.* That would be the rudest way possible to say get out, as someone would talk to a dog."

"Are teachers allowed to speak to students that way?"

"No, I am a custodian, and I know that. If this teacher had spoken to me that way, I would have told him the same thing."

"Your honor, I pass the witness in case the defendant wants to ask her any questions."

"No, I am satisfied. She is telling the truth."

"Your honor, there is no such thing as a small injustice. The State moves for a directed verdict of not guilty."

"I am going to take a recess here. Frankly, I am going to talk to your boss. It appears to me that you and the janitor are not helping the school maintain discipline. It will not surprise me if your boss suggests that you find another job, and It will not surprise me if the school fires this janitor."

"Your honor, I serve at the pleasure of the district attorney. He can fire me if he is displeased. I would not change a thing I have done today and will humbly accept his decision. However, I am glad you mentioned the custodian because if someone retaliates against her for her testimony, that is a serious crime and would not be heard in this court. If I am terminated, I could represent her in a civil action or in a federal case for violation of her civil rights."

That afternoon, Santiago was fired after being given a chance to withdraw his earlier motion and argue for a conviction of the student. As part of his "severance package," which he negotiated, the student was found not guilty. The custodian was assured she would keep her job based on the district attorney's advice to the school superintendent.

That same afternoon the sheriff wrote a letter to his brother, who served on the governor's committee for state judicial appointments.

*Dear Brother,*

*Today, in court, I witnessed a remarkable young man sacrifice his job as a prosecutor, which he had held for about five hours and probably desperately needed to accomplish justice in his first case.*

*When he has been an attorney long enough to meet the judicial requirements, I recommend you look him up and consider him for a state judicial appointment.*

*I am enclosing his brief resume, which I stole from the D.A.'s office. He is easy to recognize.*

*He has a faint red scar down the right side of his face and a great smile.*

*Sincerely,*

*Your Older Brother*

After five lean years of private practice in his hometown, he received a letter not from the state judicial appointments committee but from the federal district court clerk asking him to submit his resume for consideration of an appointment to be a federal magistrate.

It was true that during those five years, it appeared that Santiago was competing with the federal and state public defenders and with legal aid for the job of hardest working, lowest paid attorney in West Texas, but he also earned a reputation as an honorable and indomitable champion of fairness. During college, he had met and married a most supportive and wonderful woman. Hanna. His world.

At his preliminary interview for the federal magistrate, he appeared before a committee that would make its recommendation. The committee's chairman was missing through most of the interview and arrived just as the committee was about to give Santiago a polite dismissal. Santiago was standing up to leave when the chairman saw his face clearly and saw his faint scar and said, "Wait, I know you. Please sit back down. I believe you spent some time as a prosecutor."

With a huge smile, Santiago replied, "Yes, sir. That is true."

His federal background check seemed to be unending because of his ties to Mexico, but ultimately, he served as a federal magistrate for two years and then was appointed to be a federal judge.

His eyes opened. He blinked once, made the sign of the cross, and slid off his side of the bed quietly so as not to wake his beautiful Hanna. The Honorable Santiago Landeros was awake for the day. From between the master bedroom and his daughter's, he summoned a Malamute pup from its open pen with a hand signal and proceeded downstairs through the kitchen where he flipped on the coffee maker and flipped off the slow cooker which overnight had prepared everyone's lunch for that day. The dog went into the backyard for his business. Santiago entered his workout room and changed into jogging clothes, and picked up the leash for Pewee. It occurred to him that the dog had grown since they were upstairs.

It was 5:05, Friday morning. They power-walked through the neighborhood for twenty minutes, then returned to the kitchen for Pewee's breakfast and Santiago's first cup of coffee. He showered in the bathroom attached to his study so as not to wake his beautiful wife, Hanna, and then chose his suit, shirt, and tie from his walk-in closet in his study. He re-polished his shoes and chose a colorful pair of argyle socks—- his wild Friday tradition.

His wife and daughter would wake at 6:00, so he sat at the desk in his study to review each of the cases he would hear this afternoon. The defendants were all detained and would be transported by the U.S. marshals. For some unknown reason, the prisoners were awakened at 4:00 for their afternoon appearance. Each of the four had agreed to a plea earlier and would be sentenced this afternoon. A fifth prisoner was to enter his plea late in the afternoon. He should have, like the others, already entered his plea and been ready for sentencing this afternoon, but his lawyer failed to appear at the last setting without any explanation or even a phone call. Anyone who had ever missed a setting before this judge would not want to miss another one.

Personally, he could almost not be insulted, but when it came to the representation of defendants, he expected a great deal. It was the same with respecting the authority he had. No one was allowed to stand in the way of his sense of justice. In this one regard, he was indomitable.

Still sitting at his study desk, he quickly re-read every pre-trial report with the recommendation of the federal investigators. He re-read the reports of the arresting agency, the prosecutor's summary of the case, and all motions for leniency and requests for the judge to request or suggest to the Bureau of Prisons placement in a nearby penitentiary to enable family visits.

The rinse cycle had just finished, and he transferred some of this week's laundry into the dryer located beside the kitchen. He heard arguing as his wife and daughter came down the stairs, continuing where they had left off last night.

"You will not carry your cell phone to school. Your grades have plummeted, and you are constantly angry. Six more weeks of this, and your chances of graduating in May are gone."

"You don't understand."

"Good morning."

"Good morning."

There was no response from either of them, so he said, "I have court until 4:00, possibly 5:00, but your car will not be ready until tomorrow."

The daughter thought that meant the city bus for her.

Looking at his wife, "Plans?" His look said, "This is my wife whom I love." His wife replied, "I have a hearing this morning and another at 2:00 and then home." She was a court reporter.

Then he looked at his daughter, a questioning look. "My last class is over at 3:00, and then tutoring until 3:30."

"I would like this," circling with his finger around all three of them as if with a wand, "solved before I go to work.

"Division of labor. Daughter or dinner?" to his wife.

"Dinner, definitely." She was thinking, "I have the weirdest husband, so wonderful. She was thinking about his only day in the district attorney's office and how he had come home to tell her that he had been fired and that they had to move with no money. What an adventure. They had spent that winter at the ranch in Mexico, where she learned the glory of asadero cheese on hot corn tortillas made from freshly ground corn grown on the ranch.

Through gritted teeth, "Dinner will be ready at six, Melissa. You are welcome to bring a guest."

The daughter nodded, understanding that her mother declared a temporary truce, and she was wisely accepting it.

Lunch was an easier proposition—chicken with lemon sauce and a vegetable side of ratatouille which had simmered all night or grub in the school cafeteria.

"I will put your lunch on the counter, Hanna."

"Thank you and thank you for the coffee. I had better shower and dress. See you both at 6:00."

After she was well out of earshot, Santiago said, "Let's cover this."

"I know. No phone. No car. No friends. No life."

"Not exactly. Keep the phone and lose the rage. You will use my car for today, so I will need a ride to work in thirty minutes and a ride home at 5:00. The parking pass is on a clip on the driver's visor.

"By 5:00, I will want to know that you have at least started to identify what is causing your unhappiness. No details unless you want— just that you have started. If possible, I would like you to observe my last case of the day. Your opinion will help me.

"Finally, I will mention that with God's permission, your mother and I would go into southern hell to save you. We'd bring extra cans of gas for the return trip, but we have to hear the GPS lady's directions so you cannot whine."

"I don't whine."

He put up his hand like a stop sign. He signaled to the Malamute pup to sit beside him.

"Say it again."

"I don't whine."

The pup howled. He nods to him, "Sustained. I taught him that."

"Very funny, Pop."

"Remember, you have an invitation to visit Tio Diego at the ranch this summer after graduation. Two worthwhile goals." They both smiled.

The morning docket was a mixture of everything, a status review in a civil matter, one parole violation, magistrate warnings, shared evenly among all the federal judges and magistrates, and a judges' meeting. As the newest judge, he had nothing to say and hoped he would not live long enough to have to speak at one of these meetings.

The sentencing hearings started at 2:00. Four cases. Each tragic. Each defendant agreed to a tough, but fair sentence worked out between the assistant U.S. attorney and the defense counsel. Three were repeat drug trafficking offenders with large loads. In each case, the prosecutor read the summary of the case, and the defendant had an opportunity to comment on the facts but, at some point, had to admit guilt clearly. One asked permission to apologize to his family members who were in the courtroom. Two stated that the arresting officer's reports were wrong in some aspects but said that they were still guilty. The assistant U.S. attorney tried to deny allegations of inaccuracy even if ultimately inconsequential, but the judge kept them in mind and kept the agent in mind who had sworn those facts were true. The court was aware that when state agents work in conjunction with federal agencies, the state agents want to do a good job and sometimes try too hard to impress their federal supervisors.

Each of these defendants had lost a valuable load that had not belonged to him and felt safer in a minimum-security prison. As each defendant was sentenced, he was allowed a brief goodbye to his family. The officer whose accuracy was called into question was on loan from a state agency. He even tried to prevent these brief encounters, and the marshal had to make him stop interfering. The judge noted this, too.

At 4:00, the courtroom held the judge, the prosecutor, one U.S. marshal, the court reporter, the difficult officer, and the defendant sitting in the jury box. The very tall courtroom door opened, and the judge's daughter entered. Only the judge knew her. The state detective approached her and, without any authority, told her to leave since she had no business before the court.

Melissa quietly explained to the overzealous law enforcement officer in crisp, short sentences that this was an American courtroom, that she intended to stay, that if he did not like it, he could take it up with the judge, but that she knew for a fact that the judge did not like whining. All that was followed by a serene smile.

Everyone else in the large room only saw a pretty girl smiling pleasantly and a suddenly furious officer. He was very angry and told her she should learn respect.

Melissa asked him, "Do you dislike all women or just all the ones you have met so far?" This, too, was done in a quiet voice and accompanied by another pleasant smile provoking the officer's rage further.

Without identifying her, the judge asked her to take a seat in the jury box and thought, "Torturing deserving people seems to be therapeutic for her." She sat at the opposite end of the box from the young, shackled prisoner with the U.S. marshal between them.

The assistant U.S. attorney rose to ask the judge for a continuance since the defense attorney was not present. The attorney correctly stated that the continuance would not harm the defendant's case, although he would have to remain in custody. The judge liked that the attorney had not speculated where the defense counsel was—no cheap shot.

The defendant himself asked permission to speak. When given permission, he said, "May I stand?"

"Of course, but keep in mind all the rights I told you earlier."

His ankles were shackled with a chain that made normal walking impossible. His wrists were handcuffed to a tight chain around his waist. He appeared to be in his early twenties with short brown hair, brown eyes, and a light, athletic build. He was now standing before the judge in a maroon jumpsuit with the marshal beside him.

"Your honor, counsel." Santiago thought acknowledging the prosecutor was a nice touch. "I have been shackled like this since 4:00 o'clock this morning. No food, no bathroom break. This is the second time this has happened with good reason. It is now 4:04. Possibly the court could allow six more minutes before ruling on a continuance. During those six minutes, if certain things happen, I can prove to the court and to the prosecutor irrefutably that this case should be dismissed. I could even take a quick restroom break within those six minutes."

"Your honor, this case involves a family drug conspiracy, corrupting a younger brother, and brazenly using the postal system for drug delivery. I object to this defendant's testimony without his attorney."

"Overruled for the moment. Six minutes including his overdue bathroom break."

The enthusiastic state officer stepped forward to escort the prisoner, and the judge said, "No," to him. "Marshal, please." The report the judge reread this morning was written by the angry officer, and the judge wanted no opportunity for the angry officer to attempt to intimidate the prisoner.

The defendant was back before the court with the marshal beside him and about to begin when the courtroom door opened, and now two men in mail carrier uniforms tried to enter. The still very angry officer tried to prevent their entry. The defendant looked very relieved about their arrival.

Santiago was curious and ordered all three before the bench. One of the carriers asked the officer to sign the receipt for a large envelope that had been addressed to the officer. It had never been picked up despite several attempted deliveries.

Melissa and the prisoner watched this small scene unfold. The officer muttered, "I don't have time to sign for some damn envelope in the middle of the court." But he did then sign. The envelope was addressed to him.

The prisoner seemed to understand the significance of this mail delivery and began to visibly relax.

Everyone could hear the postal worker explaining how people should pick up their mail. This postal worker's tiny reprimand conveyed in open court made the officer even angrier. This worker had a normal fitting uniform. The other postal worker had a uniform that was much too big for him. Much too big.

Melissa wondered what opinion her father wanted from her. This part she knew. "Much too big."

Aside from that, she only knew that something was going on.

The prisoner knew exactly what was going on. "Your honor, I have three minutes. May I present my case?"

"Yes, but the prosecutor is right. You need your attorney."

"He is here, your honor," indicating the postal worker in the tent uniform.

"Your honor, my client requests to be allowed a brief prayer."

"No permission necessary. Proceed."

Although shackled and cuffed, he knelt right where he was. His Jewish defense attorney did as his client requested and awkwardly made the sign of the cross on his client's forehead and chest.

"Remember, oh, most gracious Virgin Mary, that never was it know that anyone who implored thy help or sought thy intercession was left unaided. Inspired by this confidence, I fly unto Thee, Oh Virgin of Virgins, my mother. To thee do I come, before thee I stand. Oh, Mother of the Word Incarnate, despise not my intentions, but hear and answer me. Amen."

His English was without accent, but he added one short prayer in fluent Spanish. "May you hear the judge's pleas ten thousand times before you even hear my name."

The prisoner stood without help and began. "The detective who just received the envelope caught my younger brother with a barely usable amount of marijuana. He told my little brother that he would do time and be raped repeatedly. He was told that I would get probation if he helped set me up for this false offense since it was my first offense. My brother told me everything."

"Prosecutor, don't you want to object to all this hearsay?" "No, your honor."

"Good. Proceed, defendant."

"To save my brother, I agreed to buy the officer's small envelope and mail it to a buyer as the officer suggested. I put his envelope into a larger envelope, the one now on the prosecutor's table. I acted as if I had to look up the buyer's address on my phone and prepared two mailing labels at the post office counter. I mailed the envelope certified in front of the detective but had placed the top sticker to the detective over the sticker to the buyer after I had shown the buyer's label to the detective. That way, it was mailed back to the detective at the address on the mailing label. My name is signed across the envelope's flap, which is still sealed. Delivery, or return in this case, of an illegal substance to law enforcement, is not a crime. I hope it's not.

"My attorney missed one, almost two hearings and was willing to incur punishment by this court while arranging with the Postal Service to deliver whatever is in that envelope to its rightful owner."

"Attorneys, approach."

The defendant was quiet with his head down, and his eyes closed but looked content. Standing there in shackles, he looked free, Melissa thought.

The judge said to the defense attorney, "Forgiven. Lose the tailor or the uniform."

"Yes, Judge. Thank you."

"Your honor, I request the court to remand the defendant into the custody of this defense attorney until a formal dismissal is prepared and signed. I expect to have some other items for the court's consideration as well," looking toward the angry officer and matching his anger.

"Denied. He will be in the custody of the U.S. Marshall until the dismissal is signed.

"Marshal, are you free for dinner? Say yes."

"Pop, it will be very hard for my guest to eat dinner with all those chains."

"Please call your mother and tell her we will be ten minutes late. And that you are bringing two guests and dessert."

# THE RETIRED ENGINEER

Why he was patient with his younger brother, he did not know. His temper at his work was well known. His volatility in his everyday life was often a source of trouble for him. He would occasionally have to change dry cleaners or even his bank because of some scene he had made in regard to carelessness or poor service. It actually interested him why he was so patient with his brother and even with others in regard to his brother. Today was an example.

Every Friday, they boarded the metro train for Trey's appointment at the Institute. As they took their seats, a passenger whom Skip recognized but did not know said, "I see the little engineer has arrived." Had the patronizing remark not involved his younger brother, the passenger would never have forgotten the torrent of abuse that would have followed his impertinence.

Instead, Skip calmly smiled at him and nodded, disregarding any possible malice in the remark. Even knowing the remark would trigger Trey's weekly ritual, Skip was at peace but did wonder why.

He supposed it was because Trey was doing his best. When his parents and oldest brother died in a train accident, Trey almost immediately began to learn how to operate a train.

His parents had been patient with Trey and his disabilities and trained Skip that if anything happened to them, Trey would be the responsibility of Skip and his older brother, Gabriel. Family history and genetics indicated the parents and Gabriel would live a very long time. Fate dictated otherwise. Ironically, they were killed, murdered actually, in a train wreck.

Trey began to rock very slightly. Then he began reciting every single step the actual engineer was taking to operate the train. "First, I secure the engineer's cabin with my special key." He wore a key around his neck given to him by a retired engineer who had been a friend of the family. Skip thought it was just something the engineer was discarding, but Trey would not go anywhere without it. "Then I secure my items in the small locker provided." Each step he actually acted out even though his passenger area was not as large as the engineer's compartment. He turned the real key in the imaginary lock and placed his lunch and small windbreaker in the area where the engineer's actual locker would be in reality. The passenger who had initiated this behavior was smiling, and Skip wondered again about the profound calm that everything in regard to Trey brought him.

Just above a whisper Trey continued to recite every single step the engineer only two cars ahead was going through. "The onboard computer indicates that all doors are secured. The stationmaster has radioed that we have a clear route to our destination. The computer displays the proper speeds with recommended reductions for curves and the approach to the station near the Institute. The engineer's role is still critical because we do not have computer-assisted safety overrides mandated by Congress, the engineer's role is still very important. I am releasing the braking system." His hands were going through the steps. "And now I am accelerating slowly while leaving this station." Again, more gestures. The political commentary about how Congress had mandated the computer safety overrides but not funded them yet belonged to the script of video reruns Trey was obsessed with, and apparently, the commentary had to be repeated during the weekly reenactment of the engineer's role. Even imaginary engineers had to stick together.

He spent Fridays at the Institute, but he would watch some part of his collection of reruns of a show out of California on other days after school. In them, a retired engineer with the kindly disposition of Mr. Rogers would invite children to see how he did his job. Trey would recite every step along with the engineer and tell what color the control was and where it was located while duplicating the engineer's action. Other than that, he rarely spoke. The Institute doctors had taught Skip that Trey had a lesser form of autism—Asperger's disorder.

No two cases were exactly alike, but in his case, there was almost no verbal communication except during his recitation. Social skills were torturous for him and for people around him. Before the accident, he barely spoke but only to family members and to anyone he trusted. Dr. Handl at the Institute said Trey might outgrow the train obsession and speak more, barring more trauma. "He might learn some other skill besides engineering. With more confidence, he might find a job fulfilling. I do not know what that job might be yet."

Well-meaning passengers again today greeted him without ever receiving any acknowledgment. During their trip, he concentrated on his duties and would not be distracted. Last year the Institute had arranged a visit to the train station with a tour of the engineer's cabin, but since the train was not going anywhere during the tour, Trey had sat silently and memorized every computer screen and every gauge and dial.

The station was within a block of the Institute and was coming up in two miles. Trey was completely aware of the location of the train and was reciting the recommended speed for the approaching curve. He recited it a second time and even indicated the appropriate speed on the imaginary computer screen before him. The speed would not have been excessive except for the curve, and no one else was aware or agitated. Trey knew and loudly said the speed was excessive and should be reduced. He began to shake both hands in front of him as if drying them.

"The engineer has to reduce the speed of the train. The engineer has to reduce the speed of the train." He was in the aisle seat, so Trey stood and began walking toward the front of the train before Skip reacted.

A conductor tried to grab him— a huge mistake in dealing with someone with any form of autism. Skip could not be calm about this. He barked at the conductor, "Stay! I will deal with this." He was so commanding that the conductor did stay. The conductor, unaware of the significance of the current speed, assured the passengers, "It is fine. He cannot get into the engineer's compartment. It is locked."

Having passed through the first car with Skip close behind, Trey came to the locked door the conductor had mentioned. Reciting from the script of the memorized reruns, Trey took the key from the chain around his neck and said, "The engineer takes the key and unlocks his compartment."

As the door was opening, Skip barely had time to ask himself why a retired engineer would give any adolescent an actual key? That retired engineer had passed away, so the question would remain forever rhetorical.

The opened door showed the engineer lying far back in his chair, held there only by his seat belt, his head lolling from side to side and his eyes open but vacant. The train was approaching the curve, now easily visible ahead. There was no script, and Trey was unable to talk. He was near panic. He knew what was happening.

Skip knew too and acted as fast as possible. He unbuckled the seatbelt of the engineer and put his hands under the engineer's arms, locking them in front of the engineer's chest and pulling him out of the way. He ad-libbed what he guessed would be said in one of Trey's videos. "The engineer has entered his compartment. He sits in his chair and buckles his seat belt."

This variation from the script was a little clunky. Trey ignored the actual unconscious engineer now lying at the back of the compartment. He got past the glitch in the script and repeated Skip's words exactly, "The engineer has entered his compartment. He sits in his chair and buckles his seatbelt." Back on script, Trey now said, "The train is exceeding the speed for the upcoming curve. The engineer adjusts the speed to the speed recommended by the onboard computer. The train is now traveling at the recommended speed." These statements were accompanied by Trey's actions as seen on the videos and as learned from his tour and from all the photos that wallpapered his bedroom.

"The train is now approaching the station at the appropriate speed, and the engineer is bringing the train to a gradual stop."

The conductor was now present and using his cell phone to call the medics and the police. The engineer's key was again invisible under Trey's shirt.

Skip said to the conductor, "The engineer brought the train to a stop and then opened the door and collapsed. He said he was having a medical emergency and had some trouble reducing the speed of the train approaching the curve."

"You can explain everything to the police, including this boy's strange behavior and how he knew the train was going too fast."

They slipped away from the station before the police arrived. The block walk to the Institute was all Skip could have managed with Trey. He was a disaster. His jet-black hair, normally neat as a pin, was disheveled. His olive complexion was ashen. He made noises that were not words. He walked very deliberately as if the ground would open and swallow them. Some of the earlier clumsiness that accompanied his Asperger's reappeared.

Three staff members took Trey to a breakfast area after being told not to mention anything about trains for now. Skip was escorted to Dr. Handl's office, where he told the doctor what had happened. The doctor listened and watched a monitor that showed the staff with Trey who appeared extremely agitated shaking his hands and then folding his arms and rocking fast.

The doctor shut off the monitor. He wanted no distractions for Skip. "There are three possibilities we need to prepare for. You know the Institute has no overnight facilities. One, you will want to take Trey home at the end of the day and keep things as regular as possible, minus the train films. Two, if he really melts down, you will have him taken to the psychiatric center, the best of all bad choices. Three, if he gets through the ride home and supper, I want you both to attend a retirement party of sorts."

Skip started to say this was not a good time for any party, but the doctor nodded his understanding.

"I have been planning step three for a while. It will be prepared and transmitted to Trey's computer. He is remarkably resilient. If my plan works, this may turn into a breakthrough. There are some indications that he has outgrown imaginary engineering. Ultimately, we must find something fulfilling for Trey so he can earn a living and you can both get on with your lives. I will see you at five."

Skip went to the police station. He introduced himself and started to explain. He was briefly assigned to an officer who was heavy-handed and said he was bringing in Skip's brother for an interview today no matter what his condition was. He had not heard what had happened, and Skip was grateful. With the very last of his patience, Skip asked for the officer's supervisor.

To his surprise, his request was quickly granted. He met a man in a suit who looked very fit and had a salt and pepper flattop haircut. He had a pleasant disposition. On the way to "flattop's" office, he said, "We've been expecting you."

Skip thought, "This is surreal."

The nameplate on the desk said, Deputy Chief Elgin. On the wall, a framed certificate identified him as liaison with homeland security. Skip was offered coffee or soda. Deputy Chief Elgin listened to Skip's truthful, detailed explanation of the morning's train ride from hell. From what he had seen of police procedure on television, he would now be made to repeat his story incessantly in an attempt to trip him up. That did not happen.

Instead, the deputy chief simply said, "Your explanation of this morning makes perfect sense. As your train was pulling out, an engineer traveling in the opposite direction saw your train's engineer unconscious and reported it to the station. We were immediately informed for reasons I will explain. The station was unable to raise him on the radio but did hear everything you and your brother said in the engineer's compartment, including your explanation to the conductor. That will remain the official version of what happened. The engineer may recover.

"Their superiors have given the engineers and conductor instructions: Your brother could sense the train was going too fast and should have reported that to the conductor. If interviewed, the conductor will take credit for saving the engineer's life by getting him prompt medical attention after the engineer stopped the train, opened his compartment door, and collapsed. Your brother will not be mentioned beyond his having noticed the speed. If you ride the train this afternoon, you will see some new faces among the passengers. They will be the ones who do not speak to you."

"Thank you. But, why?"

"There is a lot to tell you, and I think you can handle it. You handled yourself brilliantly this morning, although you couldn't have stopped the train." A ghost of a smile appeared on the deputy chief's face.

"I want to introduce you to some people—first, the claims adjustor for the railroad. I asked him to stop by the Institute and then come here. He remembers you and Trey from handling the settlement of your parents' train wreck. You may recall, he has total authority to settle claims on behalf of the railroad."

"Trey didn't damage the train. He saved it."

"We know."

A man of about thirty entered and said, "Tom Upjohn. You may remember me." He had a giant ledger checkbook under the left arm of his sports coat and a most disarming smile.

Everyone sat and he spoke, "I still represent the railroad and still have complete authority to settle all claims against it. I have reviewed the railroad's settlement agreement with you from four years ago in regard to your parents' accident. My records include a copy of the court order making you a permanent guardian of your brother. I also reviewed the ongoing release of the information you signed, giving me permission to review his services at the Institute and speak with his doctor as the payor for your brother's mental health care provider. That was part of the settlement of your parents' claim, and it is continuing. My job is to decide the cost of additional long-term care your brother will need because of the trauma he has suffered in saving the train. I will tell you he saved passengers' lives and saved us millions at great personal expense. That has gone into my calculation of what he should be compensated for.

As Dr. Handl apparently told you just before meeting me this afternoon, he was close to breaking away from his compulsive disorder until today. The doctor said Trey's prognosis is permanent institutionalization unless he overcomes today's events. In short, he needs a new career or permanent hospitalization. The Institute's best guess of the cost is also reflected in the amount I am offering you in the final settlement. The settlement offer was approved this morning before I came here. I carry this giant checkbook as a prop. Sadly, the railroad board knows exactly how much a very similar wreck cost four years ago. I will wire the settlement amount into your trust account for Trey if it is acceptable to you. You need to sign the agreement here, which includes non-disclosure. Respectfully, the railroad does not want anyone to know that Trey operated the train."

Skip had already set aside enough for Trey's lifetime care in the event of permanent hospitalization. The amount being offered by the railroad adjustor was double that.

Tom Upjohn accepted the signed settlement agreement back from Skip and said, as he was leaving, "You keep the money, even if he totally recovers. He keeps his key, too."

"There will be two more people here to help me answer questions you haven't even thought of yet."

Two men entered the room and introduced themselves. "Rob Hardy, FBI."

"Jordan Graham, Homeland Security."

They wore dark suits with dark ties, white shirts. Their shoes really shined. Trey would approve. They appeared to be in their mid-thirties, five or six years older than Skip. They carried no paper.

"Of course, you remember the extensive investigation four years ago regarding the train wreck that killed your parents and your older brother. Before you took over the photography business of your parents, investigators poured over everything in their photo studio, in their lives, and even in your home to see if they were the targets of the train wreck."

"Are you saying that train wreck was not an accident? And my brother?"

The FBI agent was speaking. "We believe your parents were murdered in that train wreck. Everyone else, including your brother, was collateral, sadly disposable. I led the national security investigation. Knowing you and your brother were on the train today, we scrambled back into action when we heard the 911 call from the other engineer."

"Wait. He didn't say our names. He doesn't even know us."

"But we do. There is a lot more to cover, but for now, you should know we think your parents died on orders from a foreign government or at least a former foreign agent. It appears that whoever caused the train wreck thought the passing of four years would make today's event appear to be another accident.

"We have been following you and your brother since you suddenly left the train. We are not interfering with your brother but have been in touch with the Institute to keep him safe."

Jordan Graham from Homeland took over. "As part of an espionage investigation, we observed Trey at the institute on a monitor in Dr. Handl's office. Your brother is apparently having a tough day because he more or less understands that what he did today was real. His pleasant, harmless illusion of operating a train has been destroyed. The doctor said Trey has nothing else for the moment to give him any structure. His illusion may have been created to prevent another wreck. Having accomplished that, he is now confused."

Deputy Chief Elgin now explained another reason for the meeting. "By yourself, you could disappear. You really are normally...looking." Another small smile. "To put you and your brother into any protection program would be difficult. He stands out. But we are working on that. He may be the target. He may have information he is not aware of. One agent or cell was thwarted, but even if the immediate threat could be eliminated, a foreign government agent might not stop."

Most of the train ride home from the Institute was its own kind of train wreck.

Skip had visited with the staff at the Institute for over an hour, from four to five. One of the staff stated, "Trey's motherboard is fried or maybe just temporarily overheated."

Trey's obsessive-compulsive behavior normally drove him to be extremely neat in his appearance. When an article of clothing became too small or too worn, it would be neatly folded and put outside his bedroom door in anticipation of replacement. He was fastidious about bathing and trimmed his hair himself very carefully. He shaved as needed. His shoes were always polished.

This afternoon his hair was disheveled, his shirttail was out, and generally, he looked like he had been in a fight and lost. Totally agitated, Trey constantly snapped the fingers of both hands in front of him as if trying to dry them. He jumped up from his seat only to sit back down again. There was no talk of what the engineer was doing. Most of the others on the train were regulars and tolerated Trey's recitations of engineer protocol. Today they had no comments about how the little engineer was doing since Trey's meltdown was so obvious. The assigned observers also stayed out of it.

The Institute did not house patients. If Trey became totally out of control, he would be taken to a hospital for temporary observation and for a three-day commitment if warranted. Skip knew that would only make things worse.

Trey was sitting in the aisle seat when he was sitting at all, and Skip was leaving him space by sitting beside the window, leaving a vacant seat between them. The same conductor was present but distant, finding that his duties called him mostly to other cars this afternoon.

Halfway through the ride, a child but not exactly a child— she was about eleven, with dark pigtails —came from the back of the car and sat between them. It seemed odd to Skip since there were not many people in the compartment, and this seat was probably the least desirable one on the train this afternoon. She wore a white blouse, khaki skirt, and white socks with brown penny loafers.

She had been trained partly by nature and partly by her mother. She had learned that a person with any brain disorder responds best to short, clear commands. She had learned that young people respond best to the voice of someone near their age. Without introduction, the girl got within inches of his ear and hissed, "Trey, stop!" And he did. He sat and did not get up again.

Each time he would start to get excited, she would say, "Breathe!" and then, "Breathe again!" She spoke with uncompromising authority.

Since she was certainly doing him no harm, Skip's overall sense of calm in regard to Trey slowly began to return, although he wondered how she knew his brother's name. Skip thought she could be in a training film for drill sergeants and thought with her coal black hair and olive skin, she could pass as their younger sister.

Most people with Asperger's avoid all eye contact. Trey certainly did. He did not need to look at her. He *knew* she was there. Each time panic would start to set in, he was aware of her again and breathed.

His intensity was still very high. Skip thought he might explode. When all surprises appeared to be over, the young girl leaned close to his ear and whispered, "Trey… Cry… Now!" The dam burst. He closed his eyes and did not move at all. He had not cried at their brother's funeral or their parents' funerals or any other time as far as Skip could remember. But he was crying now. Tears poured down his face, dripping off his chin onto his powder blue shirt and onto his dark slacks. The girl sat as still as Trey, as still as Skip. She did not speak, looking straight ahead. They all three simply ignored the other passengers and their reactions.

The thought of whether extended crying could cause dehydration lightly occurred to Skip, but now it was over. Trey's breathing was more and more regular, and each breath was deeper, and he was at peace.

Possibly sensing Trey's composure, and without another word, the girl stood and returned to her mother at the rear of the car on the opposite side of the aisle. Skip looked back, but the headrests of the seats hid the girl from view. He could see the mother and their eyes locked for less than a second. He was sure he had never seen her before.

The mother of the little drill sergeant stood to escort her daughter off the train. The exit was directly behind the seats of Skip and Trey. As she passed, she said, "Call your brother."

Certain extra people on the train saw the child and her mother and saw her whisper something to Skip. Even if they had heard, it would have made no sense to them. It barely made sense to Skip. Trey had no phone, and Gabriel had been dead for four years. Skip would call after he fed Trey and created an activity for him this evening. The Institute was miles ahead of him on that score.

Normally, he would watch engineer reruns until he got sleepy, then he would lay out his clothes for tomorrow. Reruns were probably not a good idea tonight, but the Institute had created a plan. The doctors, and his doctor, in particular, Dr. Handl, staffed each child monthly and also when a special need arose—today certainly qualified. A program had been prepared and e-mailed to Trey's computer. It was a retirement ceremony for an engineer's apprentice who drove the train when the engineer got very sick. This program thanked the apprentice and even programmed the apprentice's decommissioning.

It copied the old engineer reruns style, used the train as a backdrop, and showed what the apprentice had done and how naturally he would be upset. It explained that all this was normal when this sort of thing happened. The film walked him through a checklist of instructions to lead him from panic to peace in a voice similar to that of the old engineer who had done the television shows: "Now the engineer's apprentice turns the train back over to the engineer who has recovered." "Now the engineer's apprentice practices breathing regularly, knowing that everything is back to normal." "Now the engineer's apprentice settles back in his seat and enjoys the ride as a passenger; he's earned it." All standard procedure when any teenage apprentice drives the train and saves the passengers and the train.

Trey watched the same "retirement" clip over and over until bedtime. He walked through the living room in his pajamas without speaking, which was his customary signal that he was going to bed. He went to his room, turned on the night light, and turned off the lamp. Skip thought it was amazing that Trey could sleep and that he would not have to nap all night in a plastic chair in the waiting room of the psych center. *Thank God for the Institute and for the little drill sergeant.* That's where he'd seen her before — at the Institute with an autistic child. Now for that phone call.

His brother's phone had not been recovered from the train wreck. Two months after the funeral, Skip was in the process of deleting his brother's number but called it first out of some sense of loyalty. Gabriel's message told the caller that he was unavailable, which registered with Skip and instructed him to leave a message. He did. About once a month since then, he called and left a message for his brother, giving updates on Trey and on the photography business of his parents. He had no idea who had the phone or why it was kept turned on. His brother had become a photographer also and had lived a very private life across town for several years and was only on the fatal train to join his parents for their anniversary celebration.

The phone rang five times without going to a message. Then someone picked up.

"Hello?"

"I don't know what to ask you, except why do you have my brother's phone?"

"It's my phone. My husband left it here when he went to meet your parents. I call the number myself sometimes to hear his voice. I hope you are not offended that I listen to your messages."

"I don't know why, but I'm not. Somehow it seems appropriate. I didn't know he was married. Or that he had a child. Bossy little thing."

She laughed. "After Gabriel died, I became licensed as a foster parent to stay busy. One of the children had autism. My daughter, Josephine, mostly known as Cookie, learned to work with him at the Institute he attended weekly.

"All the foster children are gone now. There are things about to happen we cannot talk about on the phone. We must meet."

"Ok, but what's your name?"

"We will meet. Thank you."

Saturday, the day after no train wreck Friday, consisted of Skip catching up on the photo and graphic design requests for original wedding invitations and other less joyful events. He was often asked to prepare funeral notices. That included families choosing pictures for the obituary and his occasionally writing the obituary.

His biggest contract was inherited from his parents along with their house located in the old historic district. The association for the district paid him to research the original deed of every prominent historic house. The nearby university had become the repository for the county deed records. About a third of the houses had been researched at the time of his parents' deaths. In addition to the deed work, which was paid for automatically by the association, each property owner could order calling cards, envelopes, and stationery with the address of the property and a picture of the historic house. The owner could provide a picture to be placed either opposite the address at the top of the letter page or as a very light background covering the whole page.

Some pictures were provided by the historical archives of the university library. Some pictures provided by the owners contained Model A's or Model T's in front of the houses. Some had horses tied to posts with trees in wide parkways, the branches of trees from both sides almost meeting in the middle. Some had pictures of former residents going off to different wars. If no pictures were provided, Skip and Trey would go to the address and photograph the house. Occasionally the owners would ask Skip to brush out objectionable additions or "cut the grass and trim the bushes" in the photo. Virtual landscaping.

One month before the train wreck, Skip attended the monthly meeting of the association with his parents. An angry property owner objected to any pictures of his house being made public and demanded the university and Skip's parents delete any pictures in their possession. There was an old picture of him as the owner in front of his new house. His parents agreed, but the university said it could not destroy public records but would not publicize any of his house pictures. He was strangely cordial with this arrangement, and Skip thought that was as odd as his original behavior.

They were back from one of these photo shoots by eleven, and they had barely closed the front door when the doorbell rang. It was the diminutive drill instructor. "I am here to help Trey make lunch. My name is Cookie. You are my uncles."

The foyer where they all three stood had been designed by Skip and Trey's father and built with Skip's help. Their father had been a carpenter and master contractor in his homeland of Estonia before he took up photography. This peculiar remodeling of the foyer was finished two weeks before the fatal train wreck. There were two doors from the foyer into the house.

One door led into the living room area, and that was perfectly normal except for the giant lock. The other door led into a very small room their father humorously called the "guest room." This guest room had an entrance door from the foyer and a rear door on the opposite side of its entrance, but the rear door was a fake. It was actually embedded in the concrete that made up the walls.

Cookie started to enter the "guest room" since the door was opened slightly, but Skip explained to her that the room did not lead anywhere, so she and Trey went through the other door and toward the kitchen at the very back of the house. Trey accepted her as if she had always been there, as if she were part of the furniture. She had a backpack with the ingredients for lunch and a video showing how to make it. The video voice was that of Cookie's mother.

Skip was leaving the foyer himself when he saw the front doorknob being turned from the outside. He stepped into the living room, turned on his phone, and locked the door behind him, a strange feature his father had installed, a lock on the door from the foyer into the living room.

He heard voices from the other side of the door, in the foyer. "We'll kill the older one first, then the retarded one." He heard them try the door he had just closed and locked. The doorknob turned, but the door would not open. The intruders apparently then decided on the door leading into the "guest room." The fake door at the back of the "guest room" was embedded in the concrete wall but had a lit glass pane, giving the appearance that the light was coming from further back in the house. The final fortunate feature of the "guest room" was that the door leading into it from the foyer was spring-loaded. It would close and lock when the rear door was touched. This is exactly what happened, and despite smashing and banging, the intruders were unable to escape the guest room.

"May I please speak with Deputy Chief Elgin. This is an emergency. I am supposed to speak directly to him. My name is Skip."

"One second."

"Elgin here." It really was only one second.

"Did you send two men to my house?"

"Yes."

"Well, this is strange. I have two men trapped in a room in my house. Do your men speak Russian or Estonian?"

"No. Hmm. Please, open your front door slowly."

"Well, then, not strange. I see two well-dressed, well-armed men. So, the first two are very angry home invaders who were talking about killing my brother and me."

A SWAT team and a group called the Violent Criminal Apprehension Patrol were also tactically deployed all over the house's front lawn. Skip had recorded on his cell phone the threats made against him and Trey in English and Russian or probably Estonian and replayed the threats to the two teams. Jordan Graham from Homeland Security was present and took clear charge. An apprehension officer opened the "guest room" door just enough to throw in a stun grenade. The result was undoubtedly deafening inside the small concrete room but surprisingly muffled in the foyer. The apprehension team took the two men now in handcuffs to what looked like a black, unmarked ambulance for transport. The invaders were appropriately stunned and very quiet while they had their rights read to them, pointlessly since they would not be able to hear for a while. They were each given cards with their Miranda warnings on them. For a start, they would each be charged with burglary for entering the house with intent to commit a felony. From the "guest room," the police retrieved gloves, a garrote device of piano wire with wooden handles for strangulation, guns, knives, and very frightening —two body bags.

The deputy chief would arrive at three on this otherwise lazy Saturday afternoon. Meanwhile, Skip excused himself from the front of the house, relocked the door to the living room, and concentrated on Cookie and Trey in the kitchen. Oblivious of anything else, they were putting the final touches on lunch— tomato-based Fideo soup with avocado slices and shredded cheese and grilled chicken strips prepared earlier by Cookie's mom. Cookie asked if she could invite her mother since there was plenty. Skip agreed. Skip's phone was still with the police, but Cookie had a phone.

After a delicious lunch, Cookie (never called "Josephine" except by her mother) volunteered to do the dishes. Trey retired to his room.

They were left alone in the dining room. "I have about an hour and a half before a deputy chief of police comes here and tries to explain who killed my parents and your husband Gabriel and why whoever it is wants to kill Trey and me. I hope you will stay. Another compelling mystery is what your name is. 'Cookie's mom' is cool but limiting."

She smiled. "My name is Linda. You know Gabriel was a very private person. He thought that something he had done or photographed had put your family in danger. You have never heard from me because until recently, I thought the train wreck was meant to kill Gabriel. I, too, thought it had to do with his photography. I was afraid to get near you. I heard from a neighbor about yesterday morning's train incident and knew it was starting again and that you two were the targets."

Cookie came in and said she had finished cleaning up. Trey came in and wanted to show her something in his room but would only make gestures. Cookie just stared at him. She said loudly, "Trey. Speak."

Copying her style, Trey said loudly, "Come!"

"Great. Now we will have the battle of the drill sergeants."

While Trey and Cookie watched Trey's retirement film, Skip told Linda that he thought he finally understood what someone was after.

By the time Deputy Chief Elgin arrived, Skip had located everything he needed. First, of course, everyone had to be introduced. Then everyone watched the engineer retirement ceremony video. Now that Trey had seen it a few times and with Cookie, he could have pride without fear or confusion about what he had done.

Cookie thought Trey could be reprogrammed as a cook. Just follow the videos step by step. When she announced this, Trey made flickering eye contact and seemed to approve. They were excused and went to the kitchen to begin his new career.

Skip laid out his explanation to the deputy chief. "It never was about foreign governments. As you know, my parents came from Estonia, a country that Russia had horribly oppressed until its liberation. An entire museum in Tallinn is dedicated to the hundreds of ways the KGB spied on the people. One of the ex-KGB, if there is such a thing as an ex, bought a house in this historic district. His picture was taken in front of his house and placed in the university archives, and his true name, Rasmus Maksim, was used on his original deed. He wanted his children to grow up without knowledge of his past deeds, so to speak." Small return smile for the deputy chief. "This man was willing to kill trainloads of people and me and my brother yesterday to get what he wanted. The university has his picture, and I have his true name and address."

The chief radioed Graham and Hardy of the FBI, and within minutes teams of agents were back at Maksim's house and reporting back to the deputy chief. "He has vanished. His family is still in their house. We will keep surveillance teams on this house until the two invaders confess and the neighbor mastermind is apprehended. It might take a very long time. The

FBI will be handling most of this. The first two agents you met at the front door tracked the invaders from that house. They were preparing to make their entry when the two invaders went into your "guest room." Your father must have anticipated danger and wanted to make this house safe.

"May I speak with Trey before I go?"

"Of course, but he probably will not speak."

"I know. Doctor Handl has briefed me."

Trey was reluctant to come to the meeting until Cookie broke it down for him. "Trey." "Now." The deputy chief thought Cookie's command style would be very useful in dealing with a few of his subordinates. He then covered what he wanted in short order. He tapped himself on the chest and said, "Deputy Chief Elgin." Then he tapped his thick card, which was on the coffee table, and said twice, "Danger, help." Then he gave Trey a rich, red chef's apron with his card sewn onto the inside top, right at chest level. Again. "Danger. Danger. Help. Help," as he tapped the thick business card attached to the apron. "Just tap the card, and I will come running."

———•———

After two days of really hard amateur police work by Trey, Deputy Chief Elgin was invited back. Skip answered the door and was surprised that "Elgin" had been summoned. First, Trey took them to his computer and pointed at the part of a documentary on bluebirds that explained how bluebirds or blue jays robbed other nests and stole items to make their nests.

Before they could say this was not the best use of their time, he took them to the kitchen window at the back of the house and pointed to a vibrant colored bluejay in a tall tree in the backyard. Then he took them outside under that longleaf yellow pine and showed them two pieces of coated electrical wire directly beneath the bluejay's nest. The wires were different colors, and the ends had been skinned for connection. He did not touch the wire but closed his eyes and sniffed to show a clue was being presented. Then back at his computer, he showed them where those pieces of wire fit on the diagram of the bomb on his screen.

Doubtful, but to be sure, Elgin brought in the bomb experts from Homeland. The wires tested positive for exposure to explosive material, so more security was added to protect the house. Jordan Graham from Homeland Security was advised and soon appeared. The question for him was why Maksim wanted to harm them now. His identity was now known, and his past as well.

"This fits a pattern we have seen all too often recently. Former dissidents who otherwise pose no threat now are still looking to settle old scores—pure revenge. He wants you dead for knowing his identity. If it is just this agent's personal agenda, it will end when he is caught or disposed of." Skip and Elgin listened to this and so did Trey, who gave no indication that it was registering with him.

One of the FBI agents said she had never staked out a bird before, but the agency expert showed her team the approximate range in the neighborhood.

While some agents tracked the type and source of explosive material, others eliminated house by house where the bomber could be. A tip identified a house two streets away for sale, which had stood vacant for months and which had an attached garage where the light was reported shining late at night. The garage contained an open window which agents documented was the bluejay's entrance. A workbench contained bomb-making components undoubtedly destined for the brothers' house. Rasmus Maksim had been hiding in the garage since his henchmen's arrest. Moving blankets and fast-food containers were in one corner, but Rasmus was nowhere to be found.

Skip finally heard the message from Trey to Deputy Chief Elgin. Elgin had set his cell phone on the coffee table in the living room and only played it after Trey had retired to his room. "Elgin. Badman. Tap. Tap. Bomb. Tap. Tap. Come." He remembered Elgin tapping on his business card to show Trey how to reach him. For a reason he could not explain, it brought him peace, even the part where Trey thought he had to say "tap, tap" as part of the summons. He and Elgin had exchanged smiles but said nothing further about that except to agree that it would be like a password among them.

Elgin explained Maksim's former employees could still not hear very well but could write and talk and might cooperate and make the brothers' testimony unnecessary. Skip hoped so. The witness stand would not be a pleasant place, especially for Trey.

Dr. Handl and Elgin arranged a meeting at the Institute of all law enforcement agencies involved. Cookie referred to them collectively as the alphabet. The train ride to the meeting was silent, uneventful and disappointing for some of the regular passengers, just two brothers riding the train.

Trey had spent extra days at the Institute recently on an undisclosed project. Skip was given an idea of the project as if he had to be prepared. Skip found it odd that anyone would think he could ever be jealous of Trey. There were hints of that from Deputy Chief Elgin, along with Rob Hardy of the FBI. Today Dr. Handl was trying to prepare him for Trey's recent adventures as if he might surpass Skip and make him jealous. Thinking about the doctor's warnings and Rob Hardy, he felt more proud than jealous.

"The video you are about to see will change your life as well as Trey's."

Skip's doubts lasted nearly thirty seconds. Trey appeared in the unidentified kitchen of the institute, neat as a pin wearing the red Elgin apron. Trey could speak clearly in that same slightly mechanical drone heard in other videos prepared by him because it was a role. "Today, your cook will first help you prepare Ratatouille Provencal. It is very simple. Your cook will walk you through each step. If you start at 3:30, it will be ready for dinner. Here is what you will need."

The program walked the audience through the recipe and included small household suggestions, such as putting this colorful dish on a large ceramic tile backed with thick felt. "The floor tile your cook likes to use as a hotplate is 13 inches by 18 inches, big enough for a casserole dish. There are always closeout tiles left from big jobs that you can buy reasonably at the tile store. You can choose a color that matches your room. If there are enough, your cook recommends more tiles to make place settings after covering the backs with heavy felt."

His second recipe was a cheesy chicken casserole. "Sometimes your time is short, such as if you are painting your house. Just put the paintbrush in a plastic bag and put it in the refrigerator. Your cook wants you to know you can do the same with the paint roller. They will be ready for the next day's painting."

While "the alphabet" and Skip were meeting with Dr. Handl, Trey was in the Institute's kitchen making another video with the prearranged off-camera assistance of Cookie and her mother, Linda. Elgin, Skip, and Dr. Handl agreed that Trey had wisely kept Cookie and her mom out of the video for their safety. He had also made sure no one could tell that the kitchen was at the Institute.

Now on the doctor's monitor, Trey was walking his viewers through how to slowly cook a chuck roast after it was adequately floured and pan-seared in olive oil at medium heat and how "your cook" recommends keeping the mashed potatoes in the crockpot on low to concentrate on the gravy. "The crockpot will keep the potatoes hot but will not let them dry out. Your cook puts the crock right on the table on a hot pad or ceramic tile. Your cook puts the gravy in the glass container and keeps it on the warmer of the coffee machine to keep it hot and pourable without worrying about dropping the ladle into the gravy. It will never burn, and your cook can think about the dinner guests. The glass container also can sit on the table on another pad and remain hot for the entire meal."

Meanwhile, Rob Hardy of the FBI had joined the conversation while watching the newest video. "Where did your brother get all these household tips, and where did he learn to cook?" Before answering, Skip had to think about how his parents dealt with Trey.

"Before our parents died, Trey did not go to school. Some days our father took Trey to his photo studio, and other days when he had a home remodeling job, he patiently showed Trey how to read blueprints and use each tool carefully. He told Trey everything, first in English and then in Estonian. Our mother would preview an entire day with Trey in Estonian, and they would follow their preview of cooking or drawing. Before coming to America, she was a forger making documents to circumvent the harsh Russian bureaucracy that oppressed their country. I am not jealous of my brother because my parents taught him everything he is doing now. Once I thought they were entertaining him, like babysitting. Now I see they were training him to make a living. I am very proud of them and proud of him."

Dr. Handl spoke to Skip about what he and the deputy chief and the FBI agent had already discussed. "That fits in with what we were saying. Your brother knows exactly what he is doing. His cooking videos have gone viral, but that is not what he wants. He wants to use the videos to bait Mr. Maksim to come after him. He cannot run and he cannot hide, so he will hunt.

"He will not allow any assistant, especially his niece, to be seen in the videos. He has done a video which talks about how "your cook" will be traveling to Europe to promote the videos and healthy cooking. He has suggested Estonia first.

"You know better than anyone that he cannot just come to you and say he wants to travel."

———•——•——

Agent Rob Hardy, Deputy Chief Elgin, and Dr. Handl were already assembled when Skip appeared for an impromptu meeting at the institute the next week. Trey had been gone for nearly a week. Dr. Handl made an opening statement.

"I am stepping out of this meeting, although I asked you to assemble after I received the video you are about to see. My 'instructions' indicate that you have received a copy and that these are the only ones that exist. I am leaving my copy with you and will not participate further since your proceedings will now have to do with law enforcement. I will make myself available to Trey for therapy. He has indicated that your meetings will now be at Skip's house. Excuse me."

Skip spoke next. "Last week at what would normally have been his bedtime, my brother showed me his passport, which he had just removed from our parents' wall safe in our living room. He appeared to replace his passport and then returned from his room, dressed and carrying a small suitcase. He bowed toward me and solemnly shook my hand. Then he left. The video arrived this morning. My copy is not in English. I did not know that he could speak Estonian. A rough translation of his introduction says the video is from "Your Traveling Cook" in Estonia. He shows his passport and reminds travelers to renew their passports long before their planned departure. He indicated that since he was under sixteen when his passport was first issued, it is good for four years and will expire soon. He shows the original issue date and then what I think is a forged Estonian customs stamp for when he supposedly entered that country last week.

"Our father was extraordinary with a camera, and our mother was a master forger. They taught Trey. The background in the video is from our family trip to Estonia less than two months before our parents and brother died. Trey would not use archive film or anything from the internet since it might be recognized as stock film. Our mother taught him to work with documents, including passports."

Rob Hardy of the FBI said, "We are all getting to know each other better, so I'm just Rob. I watched the video in English when I arrived at my office this morning. I speak only English, but now I understand how to make kiluvoileib, fish and egg on rye bread. He even shows how to make rye bread. The video shows Trey in a kitchen that is not his house and not the institute. Could we watch the video together and see if we know where he is?"

The video seemed to give up no secrets. When it ended, the monitor flickered with static, and then Trey was facing them on screen in the same kitchen. He spoke very briefly. "Your cook sends greetings. Skip, Elgin, just Rob." They looked at each other and knew that Trey had heard their conversation since he had called Rob "just Rob." They also knew that he had forged the custom stamp of Estonia and that he had probably not left the United States yet. Skip was fairly certain that he knew where Trey was but did not say so then.

Rob suggested, "He looks older, or maybe he looks like he hasn't gotten enough sleep. There is something different about his appearance." Elgin said he thought he looked more determined. "Why does he want Maksim to think he has gone to Estonia?"

That question was posed to Jordan Graham of Homeland. Within a week, he had the answer and set a meeting at Skip's house. Elgin, just Rob, and Skip could not give Jordan Trey's passport he asked for. It was not in the safe, but its absence helped supply the answer. "You ask why someone would pretend he had gone to Estonia knowing that Maksim would go there and discover that Trey was not there. The answer is simple and brilliant. Trey wants us to know the players. We have video surveillance of Maksim leaving the country, and six days later, we have more airport video of his return from Estonia in the company of three men. Apparently, they are the replacements for the two henchmen captured here. We will know who they are—shortly. I do not know where Trey is, so I have transmitted both surveillance videos to the institute since you tell me Trey has electronic contact there. His plan was the fastest way to identify Maksim's men. If he had just sent for them, they would have come here undetected."

• — • — •

No one who knew Trey would have recognized him now. His tablet before him, he sat in the near dark at the rough workbench in the garage where

Maksim had hidden for a week. The tiny glow of the light from his tablet illuminated a face that had bags under the eyes, its first five o'clock shadow, and hair that needed trimming. More than that, the young face showed a grim determination. He was setting a trap for the man who had so callously murdered his mother, his father, his brother, and who tried to murder Skip and him.

He had heavy curtains over the garage window and had placed a box over it where his only company, the blue jay, occasionally entered, enticed by birdfeed. He had carefully placed one of the bird's feathers on the kitchen counter in the video. Even though he had rearranged the kitchen for security, Skip would know where he was if he concentrated.

So that he would not be disturbed, he had made an online offer for the house attached to the garage in his mother's maiden name. The realtor had removed the lockbox from the main house's front door as requested by an email he sent before coming to the garage. The offer and request had been routed through a computer at the University's library nearby. Maksim knew the garage had been compromised, and Trey hoped it was the last place Maksim would think to look for him.

An extra freezer and washer and dryer were all located in the garage and still connected. The day after Elgin had cleared the garage of any possible evidence, Trey had stocked the freezer with all the food he would need for his videos, which were part of his trap. He had created the illusion of a kitchen so that Maksim would not recognize his former hideout. There was a restroom originally for the use of a gardener. Trey could survive sponge baths for as long as his plan required. He slept on the floor on the large cotton pads left behind by the movers. Since the night he said good-bye to Skip, he had left the garage only once when his groceries had been delivered at night in front of the house next door. He paid in cash.

———•———

His email to Jordan Graham was also routed through a computer in the university's library a few miles from the garage. It was the university where the archives of the historic neighborhood were stored. Those archives included pictures of Rasmus Maksim's house when he moved in with his family posing under the long overhang of the prairie-style front porch. The university had promised never to publish that picture, but Trey had his copy of the same picture from his parents' file. They had never had the opportunity to delete it as they promised before being killed. He included a picture of Maksim's house as an attachment to Jordan Graham. The email asked when Maksim would return to the United States. Knowing Jordan Graham would not approve, he sent a blind copy of his email and picture to Maksim's wife to guarantee Maksim would know after his return when it was too late to hide his confederates' identities. Also, he would leave for Europe just as Maksim saw he had not gone there.

The picture and the fact that he and his parents knew about Maksim's Estonian history were at the center of the blind, murderous hatred which had caused so much damage. Trey was sure this was not state-related but only personal.

He shaved, then trimmed his hair carefully before the mirror in the garage restroom. He sponges bathed and dressed in his one set of still-ironed clothes for his trip to the airport. He had left his kitchen in the garage with pre-recorded videos set on a timer to be periodically transmitted to make it appear that he was back in the United States. He had also set up a motion-activated camera to capture any entry into the garage. That camera would transmit in real-time any break-in to just Rob.

On-line he ordered a ride from an airport shuttle and arranged to be picked up two blocks from the garage. He had neatly folded his clothes that he had laundered and put them in the small suitcase that had been his father's along with his laptop and his mother's Estonian cookbooks. He had just enough room for some American ingredients for his cooking show.

He carefully placed a large bandage over his throat to account for his not speaking. He made with ink just above the bandage what appeared to be the end of a surgical incision mostly covered by the bandage. He typed his instructions to the shuttle driver with an explanation for his silence. In the next typed explanation for anyone else he encountered, he mentioned that if they had seen him talking on one of his "Your Cook" videos, the surgery was very recent but that hopefully, he would regain his voice soon. His passport and the ticket which he had ordered earlier were neatly tucked into his sports coat pocket. A travel show on PBS recommended wearing a money belt which he was doing, but his money was American which concerned him.

———•———

Sleeping on a cement floor in an unheated garage for two weeks is not restful. Trey had napped fitfully on the Regional Jet's last leg but still arrived at the Lennart Meri Airport in Tallinn late in the day and was very sleepy. A folk song kept playing in his head in his mother's voice. He was groggy and thought it might have been played on the plane.

His only luggage was his small suitcase. He expected to have a fairly difficult time finding transportation to a hotel or youth hostel since he could almost not speak and had only American money. He passed more than a dozen gates since he left the plane, although he had seen only one runway and was now nearing the area for ground transportation.

He saw various men and women holding signs with passengers' names. One was different. A man about the age his father would be and bearing some resemblance held a sign with the word "Welcome" on it but also the words "Our Cook" with a large drawing of a bluejay's feather. The man did not speak at first but extended his hand to shake Trey's hand. Trey was finally won over when the man reached into his coat pocket and handed Trey a large cookie wrapped in cellophane with a message, "Eat the evidence. Aunt Lutsi made it. Signed Cookie"

Trey had typed a few phrases in Estonian during his stay in the garage. He handed the man with the sign a typed note since he did not know if the man spoke English or whether he was a relative. "I would like to go to a youth hostel." He was pretty sure he had written the note correctly. The man read the note and then said in English. "I am your father's brother, Marcus Rebane. I was in Russia when you were here last. My son, Artjom, your cousin, is in America selling educational material door to door. He sends his regards and offers you his room for your visit. Please stay with us. You will remember your Aunt Lutsi, also." Trey wondered how they knew of his arrival and wondered if detective work ran in the family.

The airport was practically inside the city, and they took public transportation to within a few blocks of the house. Lutsi greeted them at the open front door. She asked him to put his suitcase in Artjom's bedroom. While washing for supper, he removed the bandage and "scar" he had worn as an excuse for not speaking.

It was late, but Lutsi had yellow split pea soup with smoked ham and diced carrot ready for all of them. Spanakopita triangles, best described as spinach and feta popovers, accompanied the thick soup. He began considering a small video about how "Your Cook" makes Spanakopita which he was certain originated from Greece. Although she also spoke English, Lutsi spoke to him slowly, deliberately in Estonian. "Your father and your Uncle Marcus built this house. Then your parents moved soon after the Singing Revolution in Freedom Square."

In answer to Trey's questioning look, Marcus said, "Most Estonians live in this city. Two-thirds of our entire population came to Tallin to Freedom Square and sang our native folksongs non-stop until it was agreed that Russia would recognize our independence. Our folksongs are also our folk remedies. We sing ourselves back into balance and harmony with nature.

"Lutsi heard of your parents' and brother's train wreck from Gabriel's wife, Linda. Other than that, she stayed out of touch because we think all the troubles might have started here."

"Tomorrow Marcus and I would like to take you to our Old Town and to Freedom Square." Trey nodded emphatically and, with effort, said," Embassy, short walk. Also, video, maybe at Leib resto ja Aed for your cook program."

The husband and wife gave each other happy, surprised looks.

It was decided that the restaurant so popular with the locals should be the first stop—for breakfast—since it would be crowded later. The owner was hospitable and allowed the recording of Your Cook. Uncle Marcus held the camera phone.

"Your cook is very grateful for the chance to show the Estonian audience two recipes from America. This restaurant is known for its fresh, local vegetables, and your cook first will show a simple bread, easy to make, that will complement these vegetables— cornbread. The large ears of corn we have today began not much bigger than kernels of wheat, but at the hands of the Indians of the Americas, the size increased. Fortunately, I brought two pounds of cornmeal with me. One of your food critics says in his travel brochure that Estonia has no native dishes. Everything is stolen from the kitchens of other countries. Your cook prefers to say we borrow only the best our neighbors have to offer.

"Next, a recipe from the southeastern part of America which uses ground corn called grits. This dish is called chile, cheese, and grits and goes very well with your ham or different pork dishes, including wild boar. I will show you." Trey alternated English and Estonian in his presentation to make things more educational and internationally appealing. In the end, he dedicated the show to the owner, his patient brother, and his friend Just Rob. He thanked his audience and viewers and told them he came to share his heritage with them and correct a great injustice. The reaction was outstanding, and the owner went from being just hospitable to being grateful.

Next came the tour of Freedom Square. Marcus and Lutsi were very proud of their nation and proud of its freedom. A family in the square sang folksongs, and they invited the three to sing with them. Trey had heard some of the songs sung by his parents when he was a child. He surprised himself when he sang without hesitation two of the songs he recognized. One was his mother's song that kept repeating itself on his flight. It reinforced the feeling that his journey was right and just.

Trey was tired from yesterday's flight, from presenting the show in the restaurant, and from the exciting tour. Lutsi could see that, and so she handed him an index card with Marcus's cell phone number, an Uber phone number, and a neatly printed message telling the driver their address. She handed Trey the correct amount of euros for the short trip, including an appropriate tip.

Trey tried to protest, but Marcus told him that the restaurant owner had given them many meal coupons in gratitude for the international publicity he was already receiving from the popular program. Marcus and Lutsi told him that the owner wanted Trey to come back for lunch. They told him they knew he had business to conduct, and they would leave him to it but to call if they could help.

He had only his folded apron and his laptop with him, having given the restaurant owner all his remaining chile, cornmeal, grits, and the online link for ordering more.

•————•————•

He sat in the last pew of the beautiful, simple St. John's Lutheran Church on the east side of Freedom Square. The church was almost empty, and peacefulness came over him. He gathered his thoughts and first emailed Dr. Handl with his latest idea. He had very little trouble speaking to a camera, so he would picture a small camera on the shoulder of anyone he had to address. He thought of how Estonians sang themselves back into harmony, and he asked Dr. Handl to convey to his brother his gratitude for his patience and to convey to Skip that he was very proud of him, too.

Then he texted Skip and reminded him of when the three brothers had planted the longleaf yellow pine tree in the back yard. Gabriel told them how very slowly this tree would grow for the first eight or nine years and then shoot up very quickly and live probably over one hundred years. They were patient with the young tree and with their younger brother.

Finally, he emailed Jordan Graham and Rob Hardy (now known everywhere as "Just Rob"). He asked if Rasmus Maksim could be prosecuted in Estonia. Just Rob replied that the entire file had been transmitted to the embassy where two FBI agents were working with an Estonian prosecutor to do exactly that. Rob told Trey that since he did not know where Trey was, he just this minute told the embassy workers to expect him within two weeks and that Trey could testify if he was before a camera. Trey arrived at the embassy minutes after Rob's email and rattled the two FBI agents and the prosecutor who were preparing to go out for lunch. The prosecutor told a young intern named Anna in Estonian to babysit Trey until they returned, and they would work later in the afternoon. As soon as they left, Trey studied Anna. He tried to picture a camera on her shoulder, but it kept falling off.

Trey was not impressed with the prosecutor or his attitude and was not impressed with the word "babysit" regarding him. He was impressed with Anna, however. He spoke slowly in Estonian and asked her if she would go to lunch with him. She was closer to Skip's age than his, but that was not the problem. Anna was very amused that this visitor had understood and resented her boss. Her English was slightly better than his Estonian.

"I would love to join you for lunch. That is a very nice offer, but I have very little money."

"We will not need money." Still no camera.

They walked the short distance to Leib resto ja Aed, where he had taped the program earlier. The owner greeted them himself and said, "You are my guests; please put yourselves in my hands." As he seated them at his table, he smiled, "You both have very good taste." Anna suspected he did not mean their choice of restaurant.

"I would like to serve you our specialty, wild boar with fresh local vegetables accompanied by a side dish from America made by your lunch companion." He bowed toward Trey and said, "You work very fast." They both understood that.

Trey showed her a portion of the program on his laptop while their meal was prepared. Anna spoke, but not about the case. She told of how she had been on the police force and how she chose to be a prosecutor, which required her interning between semesters of law school. Trey told of his idea of putting an imaginary camera on a person's shoulder in order to be able to speak.

"How are you able to speak to me?"

"I don't know. Your camera keeps falling off your shoulder." He blushed, and they both laughed. He told her about how patient his brother is with him and that he hoped she could meet him someday.

"You mean like as a reward."

"It would be nice for both of you. If God wants it to happen, it will happen."

After thanking the owner for his great food and hospitality, they returned to the embassy, where they prepared a conference room for the taking of Trey's deposition, thankfully on camera. They had finished reviewing all the evidence when the prosecutor and agents finally returned.

The prosecutor wanted to apologize for not inviting Anna and the American witness to lunch but could not bring himself to do it. Instead, he said to Anna, "I see you have not arranged for an interpreter for the deposition despite the extra time you were given."

Trey imagined the biggest camera that would fit on the prosecutor's shoulder without caving it in and thought slowly in Estonian, then said very quietly so that only the prosecutor could hear him, "We ate lunch at Leib resto ja Aed as guests of the owner in gratitude for my humble cooking there this morning. I came to do my tiny part to prosecute a monster. I can speak if I face a camera or pretend there is a camera. Thank you."

Trey's modest and private explanation worked magic on the prosecutor. It gave him a chance to save face. He had the grace to apologize first to Anna and then to Trey.

Then, "Anna, how long will it take to prepare the exhibits and our witness to testify?" Her answer was most diplomatic. "I have reviewed all the evidence transmitted to us once by myself and once briefly with our witness.

With your guidance, we can tape Trey Rebane identifying the exhibits from the train wreck, the pictures, and the destruction and loss of lives. He can identify Rasmus Maksim and his henchmen and verify their threatening statements about trying to kill Trey and his brother. He can authenticate the airport video of Maksim returning to the United States with replacements for his captured henchmen. He will show how the bomb-making attempt was uncovered. He can identify the engineer who was poisoned and show his retirement video.

"I think we may finish by the end of the day."

The prosecutor said he especially wanted to see Trey's engineer training films and his retirement video. Every single piece of evidence had an FBI agent's contact information or a Homeland Security agent's contact information attached.

The chronological presentation took nearly four hours. Anna was asked to direct the presentation. She was granted student attorney status for the day, and that helped the prosecutor a great deal. During the presentation, he could quietly ask the FBI agents present to contact various agents in America for clarification and other documents such as the death certificates for Trey's parents and brother and pictures of the instruments that would have been used to kill Trey and Skip. The prosecutor also asked for documentation and plans for the "guest room" that had so nicely trapped the henchmen. Everything he asked for was transmitted before Trey finished testifying late in the afternoon after nearly four hours of non-stop questions and explanations.

"That is the most I have ever talked."

"I do not think it will be difficult to prosecute Maksim here. Excuse me."

The prosecutor was gone for nearly thirty minutes. Trey called his uncle and aunt and told them he would be there in less than an hour. The prosecutor returned and gave a small speech.

"I expected a spoiled, special needs child and a weak case. Instead, I have been presented with a very well-prepared case and a great witness, and an opportunity to do justice. The entire four hours of testimony have been transmitted to the Ministry of Justice in Moscow. Rasmus Maksim is still a Russian citizen. Unfortunately, the prosecutor there is even ruder than I am, but he is most aware that every crime committed by Maksim was done without the approval of Russia. That is very important, and it is best if none of us mention it.

"An agent named Just Rob anticipates Maksim will be in custody by tomorrow and deported here first, at our request. Because he left the country and returned, he is being denied entry as undesirable. Then Russia will ask for him. You, sir, are being asked to give almost the same live testimony in Moscow. You will be in the hands of the legendary investigator Alexander. Anna Neverkovic will escort you to your uncle's house and tomorrow to Moscow and afterward back to America. It will be good if you do not let anyone know where you are since there may be a danger. Thank you, Trey Rebane."

At the uncle and aunt's house, introductions were made, and Anna made arrangements to meet at the Lennart Meri airport in the morning.

"Our son will be returning from America in the morning. You can visit your cousin before your plane leaves.

In his entire life, Trey had never made a joke. "He can have my room. I will be going directly home from Moscow."

Marcus and Lutsi were hesitant to laugh, although they thought it was very funny.

The next morning Trey helped welcome his cousin home from America, and they heard about his sales and travels. He had seen Trey's cooking shows in America and had even seen the show from Leib resto ja Aed from the day before while on the plane. Anna arrived and was introduced to Artjom as the family was telling Trey goodbye.

The flight to Moscow was five and a half hours. Trey could speak to the flight attendants or rather to their imaginary cameras, but it was a little awkward. It was different with Anna sitting beside him. She told of her life and asked him questions about his throughout the flight. She was very comfortable to be with. He thought about what she asked but did not have answers.

Her life seemed highly organized and planned, and his did not until they talked about it. He always thought he was drifting. She saw a life well planned first by his parents, then by Skip, and now by him. She asked him if he planned to marry or continue to live with his brother, what he wanted to become, a cook, a carpenter, hopefully not a forger.

"I can picture myself at my house with my brother, but now that life seems very small and not fair to my brother. I moved to the garage to help catch Maksim. That was the first time I had ever been away from home. Skip needs a life, too. I do not know what I will become."

———•———

They landed at the enormous Pushkin Airport and briefly wondered how they would locate the investigator, the legend, Alexander.

That was no problem. Right off the plane, they were asked to accompany an airline employee who drove them a great distance on a motorized cart, all the way to the exit for ground transportation. Outside, next to a black, older car, was the legend. Anna spoke to him slowly in Russian. She told him she was delivering Trey to him. She took a picture of Alexander from the pocket of her business suit. Same huge man, same short salt and pepper haircut. She was so formal that Alexander asked if she had confirmed who he was.

"Yes."

In Russian, he said, "Do you want me to sign for the package?" nodding toward Trey.

Smiling, she said, "No." She walked back to Trey and kissed him goodbye on the cheek. Alexander did not think the kiss was wasted but asked, "Will you accompany us to the Ministry of Justice where we can all eat and then we can present ourselves to the prosecutor? First, speaking to Anna, he said, "I have reviewed the evidence transmitted yesterday. If our prosecutor needs something different, your assistance would be very useful this afternoon." Then to Trey, "I do not know why the prosecutor here expected a spoiled, special needs child and a worthless witness, but from what I have seen in the transmissions, those expectations will soon be demolished. I understand that you have been a carpenter and remodeler with your father, an assistant forger under the guidance of your mother, a train engineer, a celebrity cook, and a detective investigator. Your only problem that I can see is that you seem to have trouble holding a job."

Trey had nothing to say but was impressed with Alexander's dry, humorous delivery. Alexander took his small suitcase and put it in the trunk of his car. Anna had a copy of everything that was recorded yesterday and chose to keep it and her small suitcase close to her. Alexander said he and Trey could give her a ride to her embassy, where she would stay after they finished for the day. She was nervous about accommodations and protection for Trey until Alexander told Trey that he would be honored if he would stay with him at his parents' small apartment.

Over a late lunch of fish sandwiches and potato soup, it was agreed that they would go over half the case that day and finish tomorrow. The prosecutor said at the beginning that he disliked helping people from another country prosecute a Russian citizen. He was able to monitor the building of the case and make suggestions while working on other cases.

Meeting Alexander's parents that night was interesting. They told Trey that many Estonian surnames were from trees and animals. Since his name, Rebane, meant fox, they would call him that. Their apartment was very small, and they offered their room to him, but he said he would prefer to sleep in the living room on the floor and let Alexander have the couch. He said the carpet was much nicer than the cement floor of the unheated garage he slept on while trying to outsmart the murderer. Alexander turned to his parents, "He first used the old 'I'm going to Estonia ploy.'"

His father laughed and said, "Oldest trick in the book," and laughed. "Thank you for being our guest, little fox. Good night."

The next morning the parents said they were embarrassed that they could not offer Trey coffee. Alexander said he and Trey would have some at the Central Administration Okrug, which Trey thought might mean the OK district. Trey took a sealed two-pound bag of dark roasted medium ground coffee from his now almost empty suitcase and asked if they would accept it. "When I write, you will know it is from me since I will sign with a small "z" for zorro or little fox.

Anna was already at the Ministry of Justice Office and had already seen the dour prosecutor who first acted like he would be as difficult as yesterday. Still, when Alexander and Trey arrived, he told the three of them that he had stayed late and reviewed every piece of film and testimony and evidence and would eagerly prosecute Rasmus Maksim and his accomplices. The prosecutor sped up the presentation of evidence by having Trey identify exhibit groups.

"You have seen exhibits numbered 1 through 35 numbered individually, and can you identify them each?"

"Yes, sir."

"What are they?"

Pictures of the train wreck that killed my mother, my father, and my brother and 15 other passengers."

"Does each of them accurately portray the conditions on the day of that train wreck?"

"Yes, sir."

"You have identified pictures of the 'guest room' your father and your brother-built, pictures of the two men who were trapped in that room with their body bags and various weapons, and the recording of them planning on killing you both. Is all of that accurate? Do you still swear that every item you have identified is true and correct?"

He did the same with all the material of the engineer's identification and physical condition on the day Trey drove the train and with all the explosive material found under the pine tree and in the garage where Trey had stayed. By 10:30, every piece of evidence and testimony was identified and verified. The prosecutor told Trey to stay vigilant. "If I need any further testimony from you or your brother, we may do your depositions by video conference."

At the airport, Alexander told Trey, "Remember what my father told you. "It does not matter what you become as long as you are yourself."

Anna had gone inside the airport, and Alexander asked Trey, "You drove the train?"

"Yes."

"The flight to America is 16 and 1/2 hours. Let the pilot know you are available."

———•———

On the flight home, Trey was very pleased to have Anna's company. He was also very pleased that she would meet Skip.

"Do you have younger sisters?"

She smiled. "No, but dozens of cousins."

As soon as phones could be used on the flight, Trey called Skip and woke him up. "So… Skip." Then he laughed and hung up. Skip stayed awake briefly, trying to remember if he had ever heard Trey laugh.

For Trey's part, he was not worried. After all, he was retired.